THE COLONEL'S WIFE

❖ ❖ ❖

THE COLONEL'S WIFE

A NOVEL

ROSA LIKSOM

TRANSLATED FROM THE FINNISH BY LOLA ROGERS

Graywolf Press

First published as *Everstinna* in 2017 by Like Kustannus Oy, Helsinki

This publication is made possible, in part, by the voters of Minnesota through a Minnesota State Arts Board Operating Support grant, thanks to a legislative appropriation from the arts and cultural heritage fund. Significant support has also been provided by Target, the McKnight Foundation, the Lannan Foundation, the Amazon Literary Partnership, and other generous contributions from foundations, corporations, and individuals. To these organizations and individuals we offer our heartfelt thanks.

The Colonel's Wife has been published with the financial assistance of FILI—Finnish Literary Exchange.

Published by Graywolf Press
250 Third Avenue North, Suite 600
Minneapolis, Minnesota 55401

www.graywolfpress.org

Published in the United States of America

ISBN 978-1-64445-008-6

2 4 6 8 9 7 5 3 1
First Graywolf Printing, 2019

Library of Congress Control Number: 2019931355

Cover design: Kimberly Glyder

Cover images: Shutterstock

Thank you, H. H.

❖ ❖ ❖

THE COLONEL'S WIFE

❖ ❖ ❖

AT THE MARSHY, TERRACED EDGE of the great lake the beams of a fish weir creak and an upturned wooden boat screeches against the wall of the weir. If you turn toward the little village, you see that the houses are dark, their inhabitants gone to bed. A faint flash of fluttering curtain. Someone rolls over beneath a flowered blanket. Someone deeply dreaming scratches their leg. Someone's mouth is open, drool dripping onto a white pillowcase. Someone twitches, wakes from a dream, and falls asleep again. Someone snores fitfully. Someone sits down on the edge of a bed, lights a stub of cigarette, smokes it, squats over an enamel chamber pot for a minute with eyes closed, slides the pot under the metal bedsprings, and tumbles with a sigh back onto the straw mattress and back into a deep sleep.

But in one house, at the farthest edge of the village, a homey light quivers. That's the Colonel's wife's house. From the lakeshore it looks like a cross between an alpine hut and an old-fashioned, chimneyless cabin. The house is two stories high, with aging, warped timbers.

In the blackness of the early hours of night the frost begins to make its way in through the cracks between the floorboards. The Colonel's wife stuffs her hands under her reindeer-skin tunic, pulls the belt of the Colonel's old robe tighter around her, looks down at the camel-hair kneesocks and reindeer boots that keep her feet warm in the long hours of night, sighs, and walks to the fireplace.

She puts in a few sticks of firewood. Birchwood Tuomas brought over. With the sixth match the flame catches; the burning birch crackles up the chimney and condenses into a blaze of white heat that reaches for the icy sky.

She begins.

Best thing about the old days is that they're over.

But nothing's ever really gone for good.

IT WAS THE LOTTAS' ANNUAL SUMMER CAMP. I caught the bus to Kittilä and then knapsacked in to a boggy stand of pine way out in the woods between a lake and a backwater. The other girls and married women were already there setting up camp, and I pitched in. There was a pond to the south of us, all covered in waterweeds, and to the north was a pretty little wild stillwater lake with a sandy beach on the south shore. Rambling in the woods was something I was well used to. My dad'd taken a shine to the scouting movement when he was in Germany and he brought the idea home with him. Put me in the Girl Scouts when I was just seven. They called us young ones the Wolf Cubs. Taught us to be trustworthy, helpful, courteous, truthful, responsible, hardworking, brave, and patriotic.

While they were teaching us all those lovely scouting lessons, we fought and picked on each other and bullied the littler girls and learned about life. I was a gung-ho scout. I got to go to a lot of summer camps in Germany, and I learned the language while I was at it. *Juden raus!* It sounded so pretty back then, and sounds so awful now. So it was natural that the girls in our family would be some of the first to join the Lotta Svärds too. I was in the Little Lottas years before the group was even officially founded. We were a civil defense family, a role model for all Finns.

In the Little Lottas I learned how to set a table and how to crochet a lace tablecloth. After the War of Liberation—people call it the Finnish Civil War nowadays—we collected bones to make soap and dandelion roots for making coffee. I collected such a pile of pinecones that I got a star pinned to the chest of my uniform. I saved all my uniforms. After the armistice people thought they were shameful, but I wasn't ashamed. I put them in the bottom of my hope chest. It's still over there in a corner of the bedroom. The Lotta general at the camp was called the Dean. She was sharp-eyed, careful, and conscientious, and always on the side of life over death, so people thought she was a pacifist. She taught me how to make decent coffee, how to provision a thousand men at once, how to give first aid to the wounded, how to collect money for civil defense. I learned that a girl ought to be hardworking to the point of self-sacrifice, obedient, always diligently preparing for her future role as a mother of soldiers. That men should have a dash of the tyrant in them, and that they should be the moral superiors of women. That love is a battle that begins with hostilities from the man's side and ends with his moral victory, and a woman has to learn to accept that and still love the man purely and sincerely.

One day at the camp we had some free time. We could do whatever we wanted. Some of the girls read their Bibles, some sang hymns, some played tag. I went over to look at the marsh, to see what kind of berries we were going to have that year. Whether the cloudberries were blooming yet. I squeezed through some alder bushes and then the ground sank away under my feet and the whole world went sideways like I was in a rocking chair, and the great big beautiful swamp lay stretched out in front of me. I took off at a gallop like a wild reindeer and whooped like a holy roller. I jumped around and churned up the swamp water and such smells and gases rose up from the bottom that if I hadn't grabbed on to a knotty pine branch I would've fallen in a faint. All different colors flittered through my head and I saw all sorts of lights and shadows and reflections. The red-barked pines were humming, the mossy spruce trees were making a roaring sound, the rocks on the shore were ringing, and a flock of cranes shouted in the sky. I felt feverish, like my head'd come loose from my neck. I was laughing like some wild thing. I kept slogging on, splashing through the water in my bare feet, feeling the chilly breath of the marsh with my toes. Pretty soon I was wet to the waist, and every so often I properly sank into the sediment and sludge and rotting weeds and had all sorts of swamp weeds and fossils hanging from my hair, but that didn't stop me. I forgot about the berry blossoms. I was so free and full and limitless that I could feel the sap running through me and I thought, If death came for me right now I'd welcome it with open arms. I was nothing but divine, wondrous energy from top to bottom. Gnats and beetles and horseflies and swarms of blackflies were buzzing, frogs croaked their beckoning calls, and the cranes screeched like somebody'd shot them. I squeezed my eyes shut and drifted, trusting my instincts. My sense of smell pulled me to the south and my sense of touch to the west, and when the dusk started to fall I had a weak feeling and I stopped and opened my eyes, not knowing where I was. I didn't panic. Just looked at my muddy legs. They were covered in dark, bloody cuts, torn up by the sharp sedge grass and bitten by critters. My whole body was covered in silt. I was as black as a burnt-out pine stump. I felt between my legs, because it was sort of stinging, and my hand felt something slick poking out and dangling there. I lifted up the hem of my skirt and saw it was an eelworm, sucking my blood, right next to my cooch. It'd been slurping it up for a while—a fat, swollen thing. I detached it carefully and threw it in the rotting reeds. I was beat, so I went to lie down on a raft of moss, and right then I saw the world in a flash, the way it might be someday. It was a world that would be both man and woman, playful and loving, flooded with tenderness and pleasure, and everybody would be good to each other and everybody would just be what they are, not bad or good, and no words at all, just the senses.

With that wonderful vision, I fell asleep. The raft of turf carried me all night long, and when I woke up the waning moon was fading and I'd bumped against the shore. The water was pitch black and I looked down at its bottomless depths and saw the lights and shadows of the clouds, and I saw my reflection flashing on the surface. The serene face of a young, pretty girl, and a flagpole poking down in the wrong direction. On the flagpole fluttered the Lotta flag. I turned around and saw our camp not far down the shore. They were all cozy asleep. I tiptoed to the spot where we had our campfire, laid down a crisscross of kindling, lit a little birch-bark fire, and made a big kettle of coffee. When the others woke up they were pretty pleased to get around a pot of hot coffee straightaway.

After summer camp I was so buoyed up that nothing could hold me back. I was full of scouting and civil defense work. They were both based on German idealism and the German feeling of superiority, plus hatred of the Russkies and the idea that our job was to join all the people who spoke Finnish into one Finland. But the most basic thing was the holy trinity: home, faith, fatherland. That suited me. I took it upon myself to convert everybody to the religion of civil defense. I couldn't shut up about it, not even at the dinner table. My mother was rattled by me and my talk. She was a liberal at heart, a Young Finn, like my father had been when he was younger.

When it came time for the Lotta days in Kemi, I was hankering to go. My mother said no at first, but when my sister Rebekka promised to look after me, she relented. I copied Rebekka, put on my Lotta uniform, and that's where I gave my first speech, about how the fatherland is a treasure for which no sacrifice is ever in vain. The festivities culminated in a parade that included the Lottas and the handsome Civil Guards all decked out in their uniforms. The beauty and unity of the parade stirred up our will to fight and our enthusiasm for the coming war with the Russians.

My father was born into a well-off family of farmers who were also Kittilä's only merchant clan. He was the town's first agronomist and worked as a teacher. My paternal grandfather, Grandpa Fransi, died before I was born, and his wife, Grandma Elve, was full-blooded Sami. She lived to be 101. She wasn't from some shabby fishing family; she was a reindeer nomad. As a kid she used to take off on a reindeer sled up and down the snowy hillsides like a tundra princess. At midwinter, when the sun took its light and warmth away, or at the end of a cold, dark winter, Grandma Elve would sprinkle reindeer milk in the direction of the sun. I was Grandma Elve's pet, and she taught me a lot of the tricks of the old world. My mother was from Helsinki, from a noble Finland Swedish family. Mormor Hiltruuti, my maternal grandmother, had been a secret confidante of Governor-General Bobrikov, and her husband, Thoomas, my maternal grandfather, was a well-known businessman who made a lot of money and then lost it all. I don't have any memories of them because they died before I came kicking into the world.

I wouldn't have known anything about the collapse of the world markets or the economic depression that started in New York if it hadn't slapped me in the face when my father's beloved boyhood home outside Kittilä went on the auction block. My uncle Matti had been running the place after Grandma and Grandpa died. He'd borrowed some money from a fellow named Paksuniemi, an old schoolmate of my father's, and when it came time to pay, Matti didn't have the money. So that summer this Paksuniemi got it into his head that he needed a couple more rooms on his house, and that he would just take some rooms off Matti's house, in payment of the debt. I happened to be staying at the place, sipping a cup of raspberry leaf tea and writing poems in my diary, when Paksuniemi came to the property with some workmen. They arrived around noon, sawed the two back rooms right off the house, and had all the lumber hauled away in a horse cart before nightfall. And there was my father's home place left crying, ravaged and humiliated. Uncle Matti said, Only rich people have money nowadays. Skilled workmen with no work dragging themselves down the highways and all the jobs gone and on top of the shortages and the poverty there's been crop failures all these years in a row, farms auctioned off, debts taking a scythe to their fields, foreclosure announcements in the papers.

Then an idea came into my head, as clear as could be: Finland needed a tough leader, too, someone who would say no, who would listen to the voices of the poor and the people who'd been forced to the margins of society. The Communists couldn't do it. All I had to do was look at my uncle Matti. He was a Red, and all he did was sit around bawling when he ought to have picked up an ax and defended what was his. That was when I decided that the Lottas was a game I was ready to play right through to the end. But not only that. I decided we needed a harder, clearer, simpler way of thinking and behaving to bring Finland up.

So Uncle Matti lost two rooms of that handsome old house. Then, when Finland started to rise and the lean years turned to fat years again, he built new rooms, better than the old ones, and put tall tin stoves in both of them. I liked Uncle Matti, and didn't care at all that he was a Red. He had the same nose as my dad, but he was lazier. One time when I was still a rambunctious little kid Uncle Matti picked me up in his arms and took me to the woods. It was summer, and the gnats were out for blood. He carried me across a muddy pine bog. I didn't know where he was taking me, but he was holding me, and I didn't make a fuss. He talked to me, told me that I should never go to the swamp alone, that people drowned there, and animals, too, and there were all sorts of diseases you had to watch out for, like the creeping crud, and stinging beetles that give you bad blood, and lung cancer, and there were desperate thieves and child murderers with nothing to lose hiding in there, and unwanted fetuses. I started to cry. He shushed me and said there was nothing to be afraid of, but I should always remember what he'd told me.

I did remember, and after that I always rode my bike as fast as I could when I went past the marshes and swamps, which were around every corner in Lapland. When I got older, whenever I saw a swamp I always stopped and stared it down, just to show it who was boss.

That's how I overcame my fear, and little by little I started to love swamps and marshlands, bogs and bayous and quagmires.

I was born in a time of anger.

I grew to womanhood in a time of anger and vengeance.

THE VERY DAY MY FATHER DREW HIS LAST BREATH, the Colonel had been at our house to visit. I hid behind the door and listened to their conversation. The Colonel said that once the Hindenburg got on its feet, all the air power would be on Hitler's side—he had the money behind him, and he was going to give jobs and wealth and pride back to the German people, and conquer the world. Then my father said, And we're Germany's friends, aren't we? He said we could sort of fly on their wings, and set the other members of our tribe free from under the boot of the Russkies, and the lands of the Kalevala would be united in one Finland all the way to the Ural Mountains. Then the Colonel said, There isn't a Finn alive who wants to be seen as nothing more than the northernmost of the Baltic countries. And Dad said, Of course not. There's going to be a war soon, and we've got the nickel mines in Petsamo, so we'll be all right.

Even as a kid I could tell there was something peculiarish between my father and the Colonel. My mother'd once let it slip that in the Jaegers' camp in Germany the Colonel had saved Dad's life after he'd had a string of bad luck that'd driven him to try to hang himself.

The Colonel headed home early that evening and Dad asked me to take a sauna. I was his favorite daughter. We took turns pouring on the steam like lunatics and I gave his back a whisk, and then we sat swigging small beer in the sauna room. Dad told me how he and Mom went to Copenhagen on their honeymoon. Back then, of course, a young couple taking a honeymoon trip abroad was unheard of in Kittilä. In my mother's upper-class Swedish family, though, it was practically a duty. So Mormor and Mofa were for it and my grandma and grandpa in Kittilä were against it, because they were terribly religious, practically old-time Laestadians. My parents stayed in a pension in the center of Copenhagen and lived like royalty. It wasn't long before their money ran out. Dad called his sister in Rovaniemi and asked her to send money. But she told him that she wasn't going to send him a penny, that she thought he was living pretty high, him an agronomist and the rector of the dairy school and going and marrying one of his students. Then he called the only phone in Kittilä, which was at the family place, and as luck would have it, Uncle Matti answered. Matti sent some money right away, but the mail was slow. The man who ran the pension demanded the rent, and didn't understand when Dad told him in Latin that *pecunia venit*. The old man called the police and they took Dad away to debtors' prison. Mom was at the conditori at the time, buying some pastries, and when she came back, Dad was gone. So she asked the manager of the pension in clear Swedish where her new husband was. But he answered something in Danish and she couldn't understand him. She cried for a week there in the room and had nothing to eat but the pastries and nothing to drink but champagne. She thought my father had found a new woman and run off with her. Then one dark evening he showed up again, with a wad of money in his hand, and found his wife lying on the bed paralyzed. Everything was back to normal soon enough. They bought a great big Victorian-style baby carriage as a souvenir, because it had come to their attention that my mother was expecting their first child. Rebekka, that is. That was the same baby carriage that I spent my first few months in, looking up at the northern lights in the Lapland sky in the winter and the sky blue and white as the Finnish flag in the summer, whole and perfect.

When Dad finished telling his honeymoon story we tossed on one more ladle of water and sat in the steam for a while, then headed across the yard to the teacher's quarters where we were living. Halfway there, my father tumbled to the ground right in front of me. He lay there with his eyes rolled back in his head, and with his last bit of strength he took my hand and said, You are my black-haired angel. Nothing more came out of his mouth but a trickle of blood that ran down onto the dusky ground. That was such a horrible spot for me that I never did get over it. For years I thought my father's death was God's revenge against me for secretly listening to the men talking.

After Dad died, Uncle Matti ought to have taken my father's place, but instead the Colonel did. My uncle was too soft; my mother thought us kids needed a capable man to take Dad's place. She raised us in fear. Before she took the strap to us she'd always say, Spare the rod and spoil the child, and after a beating she'd say, Can you feel that in your brain? And you were supposed to say you could. And it was true. The memory stayed in my brain, and the pain in my body. She used to beat us till our backsides were bleeding, and it made us skittish girls. I was so jittery that I used to eat the beads off my necklace, chew on the hem of my skirt, gnaw at my mittens. One time when we were little Rebekka said to me, Put your little toe on top of the block and I'll tickle it with the ax. I did what my big sister told me to, and the next thing I knew my toe flew off and hit the barn wall. Mom beat both of us for that, and only then bandaged my foot. I lost so much blood that I caught a fever and lay half-dead for a week. Then when I got better my mother said, Whatever doesn't kill you toughens you up. Mom was a thin, fragile little thing. I was taller and stronger than her by the time I was ten, but I still had to submit to her child rearing. I'm training you girls to be decent and virtuous, she said, so the spirit of God will show in your character. She was deeply religious and always mad about something, always worrying after us kids, and that can affect your temperament later, when you're full grown. Her favorite saying was, If it's not necessary, then it's a sin. Which didn't apply to her, of course, just to anything us kids wanted to do that she thought wasn't proper. If we did it anyway we'd get a visit from Mr. Birchbranch. Once when I was just four tender years old, I was lying on my uncle Matti's cellar door enjoying the sunshine. I took my pants off and started fiddling with my button. My mother walked by and saw me. She yelled at me and said that it was an ugly thing I was doing and that if I ever did it again God would strike me blind. That gave me a scare, of course, and I started bawling. Then when I was a little older she gave me a lecture about how everything to do with the body was pollution of the spirit and retarded your intelligence and made you crazy. After that, whenever she wasn't looking I tried to break those rules as often as I could.

My father was given a nice burial and then I was left all alone. My world was barren and empty. In my head I thought, Am I going to die, or am I going to follow in my father's footsteps?

After the funeral there was a summer jamboree in Oulu. I told my mother the Lapua Blackshirts were calling to me with Dad's spirit, and she said, Don't mix your father up in this, you're not going. And I said, But Rebekka gets to go. And she said, I'm not letting either one of you fool kids go and make a ruckus with the fascists, there's a limit to everything, including patriotism. Rebekka stayed home, but I snuck out.

The train whisked into Oulu station late in the morning. The church bells were ringing, an orchestra was playing a march in front of the railway station, and a festive mood was in the air. The parade and speeches were scheduled to start at noon in front of city hall. I walked around looking at everything and joined a crowd of farmers headed toward the market square. Then I sat down on the steps of a building next to the square and took out a sandwich wrapped in wax paper that I'd brought with me. And who should sidle up to sit beside me but Ritva Rämevaari, my old schoolmate. She told me she was a Red, on her way to the Communist Youth camp. I said, I'm a White, but we've got a lot in common, old schoolmates plus both of us filled with a feeling of power, a longing for revolution, both burning with rebel fire. I said I was glad that democracy was played out and that the New Europe was finally getting its hands on some leaders who knew what they were doing, and that she no doubt agreed. She nodded. I offered her some sandwich; we swapped news and gossip and then went our separate ways. I meandered over to the main stage for the ceremonies. The sun shone cold in the East, and there were a lot of us. At exactly noon, two big black cars pulled up and stopped behind the stage. Out of one car, slowly and ceremoniously, emerged Vihtori Kosola, the king of the Lapua movement. We all watched in silence as he stepped onto the stage. Already waiting there were Paavo Nurmi the runner and Tauno Palo the movie star and a poster of Mussolini. Vihtori Kosola had Paavo's steady gait, Tauno's eyes, and Mussolini's gestures, and his speech went through me like a freshly sharpened knife. I was thrilled by his words—like "race," which I immediately associated with bloodlines and the honor of our forefathers; and "heroism," which to me had a whiff of the legends of the saints and the simple beauty of a Spartan soldier; and "austerity," which was about how money and riches aren't what will bring you happiness, only a belief in God and our growing, blossoming fatherland can. Kosola said that the national feeling of the Finnish people had grown weaker than the Germans' because they were intelligent and curious, and it was our job to catch up and then surpass them. When the speeches were over I was dazzled by the magic of fascism and it felt like anything was possible. Like there was a direct connection between Kosola and me and the whole audience, a line that was completely open. I bought a black shirt from a souvenir stand and put it on over my Lotta uniform. After a short break the orchestra struck up a march, the parade fell in, and we set off at a clip toward the Civil Defense headquarters or the fire department or someplace like that. I marched with hope and passion, the only young woman among all the men. We shouted that the Baltic Sea was going to become the German Sea, and that we wanted a one-party system modeled on Germany's because that was the best way to fight off Bolshevism, and that labor unions should be abolished and a Finnish Labor Front established where employers and employees strove together for the good of country, and some other things.

A wise man once said that you can only surrender once, but life has shown me that you can actually surrender again and again.

After the march the leader of our unit asked me to come with him to a nearby school because there was a picture of Marshal Mannerheim there and he said he bet I'd never seen it before. I trustingly followed him, and when we stepped inside the school building he shoved me into a sports supply closet and forced himself on me.

I was left lying there on the floor, unable to move. I was like ice from the waist down, and couldn't work my legs, or even my tongue. It felt like I'd had a big rusty nail pounded into my head. It wasn't until night fell that I could wiggle my toes enough to get the blood back into my legs and eventually stagger out of there.

I went home completely beaten, and my mother's anger relented the moment she saw the sorry state I was in, which made her jump. She asked if I'd caught the plague or consumption or what. I stumbled through the dusty geraniums and the brass knick-knacks and the Chinese floor vases all pale, with my head pounding, and told her I'd just caught a horrible flu and I was done in. We left it at that, but after that I felt like I had to leave home as fast as

I could because I felt so horribly disgusted about the whole thing. I decided I would do like Germany did and plan a surprise maneuver: I would marry the first man I came across. I thought marriage was a way to move out, to make a clean sweep, a fresh start, like the Führer did in the spring of 1930.

It was around potato-picking time. I went to the Laakkonens' one day to dig some spuds, and I saw a fellow there who lived down by the lake someplace. He wasn't ugly, or pretty. He wasn't anything. I don't remember his name, but I called him Pretty Boy because he had such a girlish figure. I married him and moved into his place, a big country house. For my inheritance I got my father's old gold-framed mirror that he bought in Ingria and my mother's old piano, which was so out of tune that you couldn't really play it, but I played it anyway. The marriage lasted from autumn to spring. There was nothing really wrong with the fellow except that he was tied to the land all the way up to his eyeballs. I thought that I was made for greater things, that the life of a housewife was too trivial for me. I wanted out of the marriage. It had accomplished what it was meant to do.

I filed for divorce around the same time Germany was breaking the Treaty of Versailles. I wanted to get back to my natural instincts, just like Germany did. But getting a divorce was like pulling teeth, and there was nothing I could do but wait. My life dragged on, and while it did the Lapua movement, and its offspring the Patriotic People's movement, started to leave a bad taste in my mouth, like barn muck. I went to the village sports club and listened to the old guys reciting their lists of the people in the village who ought to be slaughtered. They harped on about cigar-smoking Jews who came to Finland looking for amnesty even though they had plenty of money for expensive tobacco. They weren't going to let them in. And they talked about poor Jews who came whining for amnesty for purely economic and humanitarian reasons. They weren't going to let them in either. They weren't letting any Jews in. Let them go to the camps.

I finally got fed up with them after the incident with Gröönruus the writer. He ran the village pharmacy out of his house, and wrote Agrarian League pieces for *Home and Hearth* magazine. I used to go at least once a week to visit and chat with him. We'd talk about books or life. Gröönruus said that there was only one serious philosophical problem in the world: suicide. I've thought about that ever since.

One morning Pretty Boy went out to the barn and he heard a weird wheezing, squeaking sound from the muck room. He thought a pig had wandered in there, and he went to open the door and let the thing out, and when he pulled the door open he saw a burlap sack in there and noticed that there was something moving inside it, and that was where the noise was coming from. So he opened up the sack, and there was Gröönruus. Pretty Boy came to the house to get help, and of course I came running, and brought the camphor drops with me. It was a bloody sight. I said, Is he alive? He was, but he was crippled up for the rest of his life. The Patriotic People had smashed his writing hand to bits with the blunt end of an ax. I was so fit to be tied about it that I caught a train to Lapua to see Vihtori Kosola. He wasn't home; he'd gone to the party offices. So I went to headquarters and there was Kosola, hard at work planning Finland's final whitewash. I thought, Vihtori Kosola's a wise, sharp-witted man; he'll put a stop to this nonsense. First I told him whose daughter I was, because he and my father had known each other back in the War of Liberation days, and then I told him what had happened to my friend Gröönruus. I swore that he wasn't a Communist, just a harmless Agrarianist writer. Kosola listened carefully and then he said, You're too tenderhearted. You ought to toughen up, because it's ink-blackened niggers like him who are paving the way to communism. I left there in shock and decided that I wasn't ever going to participate in Finnish fascist activities again. I didn't want to be any part of their stupid marches, crowing about how the wisdom and common sense of the Finnish people were blossoming.

Kosola could keep his tacky Mussolini fascism. I would find a better, purer way. I remembered what my father used to say: that all the best things came from Germany—religion from Martin Luther, coffee from Paulig—and I added nationalism from the Führer. I gave up on Finland's cheap, homegrown fascists and set my sights on the German variety. Rebekka came to the farm to see me in the early winter and we barricaded ourselves in the south end of the attic. We read aloud to each other from *Mein Kampf* and were as excited as two crazy kids could be. Every so often Pretty Boy would come to the door and knock quietly and ask if he could come in and we would shout, Go away! We're talking about women's troubles! Rebekka read to me about how the Führer had built a fine and functional network of concentration camps where they put the filthy people. Back then the camps were a fact of life all around the world. In both the East and the West people thought they were an efficient, practical way of organizing things. I thought that progress was moving forward and that the Nazis wouldn't build the kind of barbaric, bloody places we had in Finland during the War of Liberation—and for a long while after. Germany was a great civilization. Surely they understood good food and hygiene as well as they did everything else.

I had seen my first real German at the beginning of June in 1918, as the War of Liberation was ending, when German troops came to Oulu from Helsinki to size up what they thought of as their territory. Finland was practically a German colony at the time, and my family was in Oulu that summer because of my father's work. Me and Rebekka stood stock-still next to my father at the railroad station, eagerly waiting for the arrival of these special guests.

I remember my dad's felt hat, the smell of summer berber, and Rebekka's white apron, which I coveted. A band of German soldiers gave a drumroll, marching music echoed through the summer day, and a lovely hubbub and a smell of horse manure spread over the rail yard. The train was brimming over with hundreds of Germans: officers and enlisted men, bicycle corps and infantry men who smelled so sweet I wanted to lick them. Some of them were carrying bags of wheat flour on their backs, some had sacks of rice. One soldier came right up to me and picked me up in his arms and kissed me on the cheek and whispered German secrets in my little ear. Then he stroked my curly black hair and lifted me onto his shoulders. I fell instantly in love with that big-eyed German boy, because my father, of course, never knew how to be tender with us kids, he always just moped behind a newspaper. It was on that same train that the Colonel arrived, too, coming home from his training on the Southern Front. It was his job to whip the wild, free North into shape and get it organized. Rebekka says that the Colonel and Tschirschky, who was the acting commander of the Germans, walked as far as the market square with us and chatted with Dad before they joined the German parade. I don't remember that. Dad and the Colonel had a lot in common: football in their youth, the Civil Guard movement, the Jaeger movement, Greater Finland, and after the War of Liberation, monarchism. Dad was really disappointed for a while when Finland didn't become a monarchy. He would've liked it if Prince Frederick Charles of Hesse had become the king of Finland. He thought it would solidify our relationship with Germany. But the Finnish people refused to go for it. The Democrats tricked us into democracy on the pretext that the German front was crumbling in the West and Germany had lost the First World War. We never wanted to be on the side of the losers, although we always seemed to end up there.

After the welcome marches were over, a German corporal named

Herman Suhlmann set up a canteen along one side of Oulu market, between Sutinen's chicken coop stand and Viikman the bespoke tailor. Herman had all sorts of treats that nobody'd ever seen in Lapland. I went running after Rebekka to that canteen several times a day. It was like we were in paradise. The whole town of Oulu burst into blossom. Rebekka danced at the Volunteer Fire Department every night and even I got to stand in the doorway sometimes and watch. I remember how the helmets hanging on the coatrack would clatter to the beat of a polka.

And then the Germans left, continuing east through Kajaani to Viipuri. For a long time I thought of this as a terrible tragedy. The sky looking grimly down at us, buckets of rain, bells tolling, and the soldiers loading everything they'd brought into black boxcars. I stood on the station platform behind my mother and father and the Oulu elite, soaked to the skin, as the band struck up the "Pori March," followed immediately by "Deutschland über Alles." Rebekka ran along beside the train shouting good-byes to the beloved German soldiers and officers, my mother cried, the day turned dark, and silence fell over us. Our few days in paradise were over, and life turned ordinary again, like the bottom of an empty sack a person tries in vain to scrape a little joy out of.

Holed up there in the attic, me and Rebekka sussed out what the writings of the sharpest thinkers in Finland's Patriotic People's movement had in common with Germany's National Socialists. We found all sorts of things. We Finnish patriots hated democracy, liberalism, Russians, and Communists. We were worried about the fate of a beloved fatherland on the brink of crisis, and we dreamed of an ideal nationalist homeland with just one party, one leader, and one people. A country with no conflicts, crises, or problems, full of discipline, order, obedience, and loyalty. A country with a powerful leader doing God's work, a strong nation where the individual was a cog in a well-oiled machine, where the mark of a good citizen was a fervent desire to be a model of sacrifice and renunciation, where militarism, industry, and agriculture blossomed, where a pure Aryan (in other words, Germanic) race controlled the lesser races, where life was ruled by the strongest, in the social Darwinist sense, by a cleansing, biological racial science, mass psychology, an ideology that separated the intellectual from the spiritual, a mythical and dualistic concept of history and reality, a rejection of Christianity and other religious philosophies, a disdain for feminism, and a cult of hero worship.

We figured Nazism was where we belonged. There was only one leader for us, and it was Hitler.

Rebekka went back to Helsinki and sent me books she got from Maila Talvio. She'd met Maila there and they'd become friends. As a Germanophile, Maila had many close contacts in Germany, and she'd been a supporter of the Führer since 1922. I started subscribing to *Der Angri*, which was edited by Goebbels. I can honestly say that I understood the ideas and philosophy of the Third Reich from top to bottom. The Führer had decided that Germany would produce everything it needed, that self-sufficiency was key. And Germany had everything it needed except for nickel and ball bearings and money. Which it needed for the coming war. We, coincidentally, had Europe's largest nickel mine, in Petsamo. The Führer had banned animal experiments, talked about vegetarianism and how a healthy mind in a healthy body radiated with a flow of balanced energies. All of this excited me. I had no sympathy for Jews and other filthy people. Getting rid of them was the price to be paid for a cleaner, prettier, better world. Aesthetics have been important to me ever since I was a kid. I got it from my godmother, who was an artistic person.

I could see that Germany was going to lead first Europe and

then the whole world to a new level of organization, and I wanted to help build it. The Germans had put the Weimar Republic and its unemployment behind them and were setting off toward a new, better, simpler, and more rational world.

My divorce papers finally arrived in the mail and I told Pretty Boy, very sweetly, *Auf veetersane*, applied for a teaching job in Hirttojärvi, and was hired. The teacher of the upper class was a pastor and a Jaeger and he always wore his uniform with his medals on his chest when he was teaching. He preached against Russia and the devil in the same breath. I was the popular teacher and I treated the kids with respect. I taught them that animals and nature should be treated with respect, and they understood that. Children possess an inner sense of the equality of nature and people that adults can no longer understand. I told them that if humanity were to disappear from the earth, in about five hundred years everything would be covered in wild forest. The people in the village thought it strange, of course, when I sometimes taught math or history sitting on the riverbank or the lakeshore, but I preferred fresh air to being indoors, so we were nearly always outside. The kids didn't mind. In fact, they were keen to go to school in the morning.

My father was my role model for how to be a teacher. Before he died, us kids were students in his class. He was a strict teacher, like they all were back then. I once gave a wrong answer during an arithmetic lesson and he swacked me in the ear with his pointer so hard that blood splattered out. As a father, though, he was relaxed and merciful, unlike my mother, who beat the heck out of us just for fun. Dad and the Colonel had been in the same class for Jaeger training. My mother thought they shared a bond. They were sort of cut from the same cloth, but my father didn't like the Colonel. When he had his Border Guard commander's post built across from our place, Dad wouldn't let us kids go over there. I was four then, and naturally I went over as soon as he wasn't looking. When

I got a little older I started to be scared of the Colonel. Maybe because he always tickled me after he gave me candy.

He used to come over and sit in our easy chair and dole out his truths: Ståhlberg had no understanding of the Finnish people or Finnish values, he was a shitty president and a Russian turncoat; what the country needed was order and discipline; young people were rotten to the core and lazy and had lost their moral compass with all that spinning on the dance floor and nothing was sacred to them anymore and that was why they had become tools of the devil and had rejected virtue and surrendered to temptation; and all this fawning over the Reds had to stop. If my uncle Matti happened to be visiting and disagreed, the Colonel would go nuts, roaring and threatening and eventually pulling his pistol out of his pocket. Us kids learned that the Colonel was always right and knew everything there was to know. He would shoot me a crooked grin, but he would stare at Rebekka.

When I had my thirteenth birthday party, two years after my father died, my godparents, my uncle Matti, and the Colonel came over. The Colonel had his hair slicked back and parted down the middle, short sideburns, long eyelashes, a sparkle in his eye, and a hearty smile. He had a colorful row of ribbons over the left breast pocket of his military tunic, like other men of his rank, and he wore the top button open, with loose pants tucked into *lapikas* boots. He was different from the other officers, and even though he was old, he looked handsome. He brought me a book of Koskenniemi poems as a birthday present. I loved that book. I decided that I wouldn't be afraid of the Colonel anymore. While we were sitting around the table my mother asked me to read a poem I'd written myself, and I noticed the Colonel looking at me in a very different way than before. After that birthday party he always called me "the little poetess." That look would become very familiar to me in the coming years. It was repulsive to me but at the same time it gave me a sort of a little flutter that he was looking at me now and not at Rebekka. My uncle Matti noticed, and when he and I were alone he gave me a fatherly talk and told me to watch out for the Colonel whatever I did because he was a mean, ruthless caricature of a human being who had sold his soul to the devil. I thought it was just the envious class resentment of a Communist.

The Colonel had been married to a woman named Katri since I was nine years old. Our whole family went with my father to their wedding. All eight daughters and one son. Dad picked at his nose through the whole ceremony.

That was two summers before my dad died. Then the Colonel took the reins at our house, put Mom on a leash, and sent us kids to the middle school and then to the teachers' college in Jyväskylä. Except for Rebekka. She was so afraid of the Colonel that she ran away to Helsinki, got into the National Theater school, and became an actress.

The Colonel and Katri lived at the Border Guard station, a timbered castle across from our house. Hulta Häkki, the old maid who'd taken care of the house since the Colonel arrived in Lapland, was already living there. The Colonel would come over to our house and us kids were always running over to the castle too. Katri loved children and gave us wheat rolls and sometimes peppermint sticks she'd bought in Sweden. We liked Katri. She had big, sad eyes and cried easily.

Years later, when we lived in Tammisaari during the Lapland War, the Colonel told me that he married Katri because he needed some companionship and free pussy, but that hers was so sour no seed would sprout in it.

Sergeant Alatalo, the Colonel's driver, talked to me about the Colonel and Katri quite a lot. He said he'd seen Katri's face covered with bruises many times, and that her arms were so blue from the Colonel's grip that she practically never wore short sleeves. Katri cried often. She said it was because she had no child to hold in her arms.

One summer a man gave the Colonel two bear cubs as a present. They were orphans and the man said they could be pets for the Colonel's missus. Katri was quite taken with the roly-poly things and really threw herself into taking care of them. Sometime that fall she went out on an errand and when she came back she didn't see the bear cubs anywhere. Or the Colonel. She got very worried and looked for those cubs for a long while before she found them, in the woods behind the house. They were both hanging from a pine bough by ropes around their necks. She had a nervous breakdown, and later on cancer got into her. The Colonel tried to comfort her, said he had to kill them before they killed him and her both. But it didn't help, and their marriage went downhill after that.

Mom peddled the Colonel to Rebekka for years after Dad died. She used to say, The Colonel's a good man, a respected soldier who can support a family. She didn't look askance even when there was talk in the village about how the Colonel's whores had a weird way of disappearing and his wives and lovers turned from blooming, strapping women into tottering, ghosty things. She wasn't even deterred by the fact that Rebekka hated the Colonel. Or that he was married to Katri. Five years after they moved into the Border Guard house, Katri quietly took sick. Every day my mother would say, She could die anytime now. But Katri didn't die. Finally the Colonel sent her to Helsinki, where she lay in a hospital for six months before death carried her tortured body away. I'm sure the Colonel looked in on her whenever he was in the city, although he never mentioned her. She was buried quietly at Hietaniemi cemetery in Helsinki.

This is my past. This is how I remember it.

I'D BEEN WORKING AS A SCHOOLTEACHER in Hirttojärvi for three weeks when somebody knocked at the window of my little teacher's shack in the middle of the night. It was the Colonel. I let him in. He smelled of cigars and shaving cream, just like my dad used to smell. We went straight to bed and the two of us rutted under the crescent moon till he nearly split the seams on his uniform and we didn't let up till the wee hours of the morning. With his first push into me, gravity disappeared. I floated in the air like a bird and forgot myself.

Then the sunrise peeped through the window, gray and cold. The Colonel squirmed and wheezed and breathed heavy all morning. He went at me again, before I could even get my eyes open. I was sure I'd get pregnant, but I didn't. He said no woman's pussy ever smelled as good as mine, and he proposed to me in German as he wiped his mouth on the flowered curtains.

Our secret engagement began in that little shack. First he lit a smoke, then he slipped a sapphire ring he'd got in Germany onto the middle finger of my right hand. It was engraved "Ruth 6-6-06." I was in heaven, even though we were surrounded by reindeer carcasses nearly black with flies and stomachs swollen by the summer heat. They stank, of course, but they didn't scare me. We all knew they were dying from a disease they caught from the Russian reindeer herds across the border.

We were together for three nights and three mornings. We slept in each other's arms under the open sky, marveled at the northern lights, looked for constellations and found the Bear, the Pleiades, Cassiopeia, and the Twin Boats, and I felt the fresh winds around me. The Colonel woke up so sweetly in the mornings. First he would yawn into his hand, his old man's body heavy and stiff, then he'd grab me and sweep me onto his big cock, already about to come. I admired his firm, soldierly way of making love, his readiness to die at any moment. After one bout he took out his pistol, pressed it against my cheek, and said, Take this in your pretty hand and feel its weight. Then he told me to kiss it, and I kissed it, looking him in the eye all the while, and I started to laugh. He said, What are you giggling about? and I said, You're so different from other people. He took two hand grenades out of his pack and laid one on my panties, right over my cooch, and the other one against my mouth, and he told me to grab the pin with my teeth.

The Colonel said we shouldn't tell anyone about our engagement—except for my mother, because a widow needed comfort to get through her dreary days. I knew better, but I didn't argue. The Colonel drove us down to my mother's place in Rovaniemi. She wasn't alone; my uncle Matti was there having coffee. She turned white when she saw us walk in the door hand in hand. The Colonel gave a nod and Mom and him went in the back room. I don't know what kind of deal they made, but when they came back out my mother's cheeks were a healthy red and she gave me a hearty congratulations. She said, All is well and it won't leave the walls of this house until Katri's dead and moldering in her grave.

Uncle Matti gave us a hard look, but he didn't say anything. Then when the Colonel left to go across the road and get some work done, Uncle Matti's voice shook and he said, Girl, don't you remember when I told you, like a father, that the Colonel is a tyrant? And I said, There's no stopping love. And he said, There is if you want to stop it. One side of his mouth was twitching. Think about how much older he is, Matti said. And I said, Old friends are the best friends.

The Colonel was almost as old as my father, but I didn't think about that. Age is just a number, the Colonel liked to say. And besides, Dad was twenty-eight years older than Mom, the same age difference as the Colonel and me. Uncle Matti tried telling me that he'd learned from his civil war days that being in combat teaches a man to hate. You're not allowed to show any fear, and if you do they'll execute you. He said a professional soldier has violence and aggression in his blood; he thinks it's a normal, perfectly ordinary way to be. He said, In addition to all that, the Colonel knows that there is no God and no damnation, so he's prone to seek pleasure and to become a slave to the blackest of vices.

In spite of my youth, I had sensed, and had seen, an ecstasy of anger in the tight muscles of the Colonel's face, in his talk, the clomp of his boots, the way he moved when he sat down or stood up, how he paced back and forth and twitched and jumped, how restless he could be. He didn't even try to hide what he was. It was there for all to see, and that very fact drew me to him, because he was so odd and strange. I thought that his anger would stay on the battlefield, that it wouldn't come home with him, would never come between us. That I could heal him with love.

Our engagement was a long one, and our happiness was so deep that even Uncle Matti started to believe the Colonel had changed. We often read aloud to each other in the evening from Axel Londen's *A Hunting Trip in the North*, A. E. Järvinen's *Wilderness Light*, and other books like that. Once I told the Colonel, during one of the happy times we had in the fifties, that I'd like to read a wilderness book written by a woman. And he said, There aren't any—you should write one yourself. And I got excited and picked up a notebook and started scribbling. It was easy. The words gushed out of me onto the paper. I didn't have to think at all, I just let it come. It was like a dam broke and all the words that had been waiting behind it were released. Long sentences that meandered up and down. I'd been keeping a diary since I was seven and I'd hit upon the fact that I could put things down in it as they really were—or just the opposite. I could make up all sorts of things and describe people and places in a way they never were. Writing a book was a smooth feeling, like drinking a glass of water when you've got an awful thirst. I scratched away with the Colonel's purple pen, and in two days and two nights I'd written a whole story. When it was done I slept for thirty-three hours straight. Didn't even get up to pee. While I was sleeping the Colonel read it and he praised it backwards and forwards. He sent the notebook to a publishing house and a secretary there typed it up nicely and corrected all my mistakes, and they published it. The book was praised in all the papers. Then when I started writing another book, I noticed the Colonel wasn't glad about it at all. He grumbled and didn't have a single pretty word to say. I asked him why he wasn't encouraging me anymore. He said that his little poetess would die if she took up writing in earnest. That a girl can certainly write one book, but not two. He said my writing took my thoughts away from him. And I said, That's true. When a person's writing she's someplace else, in her own world, and everyone else is sort of pushed to the background. But I didn't want to give it up because it seemed like the more the Colonel kept me down, the less there was of me. In the end the only time I existed was when I was writing. I started putting words to paper in secret, when he wasn't there to see me. If he was home I would take my notebook into the sauna. I wrote all my books by hand, right up until I moved in with Tuomas years later and I could afford to buy a typewriter. That machine was my best friend. Tuomas liked the click of the keys. He said that as soon as he heard the clatter of my keys in the evening he'd fall right to sleep.

The teaching job at Hirttojärvi ended and the Colonel established a Border Guard post a few miles from Inari and hired me, with taxpayer money, as his private secretary. I was the only employee of the post, and his bride-to-be, which meant that he could pop in from Rovaniemi whenever he wanted. I'd wait and pine for him till I couldn't eat. Every day without him felt like it lasted a year. And when we were together the hours quickly slipped away until it was time for him to leave again. When that time came, we always spoke German to each other. It was our language of love. And we would both cry like crazy kids. The sparkle of our love almost outdid the northern lights in the Lapland sky. We made love under a rainbow that ended on the purple horizon and in the rough winds at the top of Saariselkä and in the arms of an ice-clear Lake Inari night. We didn't stop when morning came, even when the Colonel was supposed to be at the garrison boot camp building boys into men.

In the very first stretch of our secret engagement I found myself in a competition with the Colonel. We were out fishing. We started out in the middle of Lake Inari and then headed into a marshy cove. We were both using the exact same tackle. The Colonel said, Let's see who can catch the most fish in twelve hours. I liked the idea, because I was an experienced fisherman. In the first five hours I hauled in fifteen handsome perch and the Colonel caught ten. At the end of twelve hours the count was fifty-two perch for me and forty-nine for him. He got so mad that he threw me out of the boat into the ice-cold water and I had to swim to shore. Naturally it was a little alarming. He acted like nothing had happened and helped me out of my wet clothes. He just said, You win, and I walked back to the fishing cabin stark naked. He thought it was funny. And I was so in love with the old codger that I forgave him immediately. I was still wet behind the ears; I didn't understand yet that the Colonel always had to win, particularly when it came to fishing.

Before the war, we used to go on treks together. He had learned back in boot camp how liberating the outdoors could be.

Once when I was at the Kaurilovi farm helping with the rye harvest, the Colonel's car pulled up at the end of the field and Jaska Kaurilovi gave me a crooked grin and said, There he is, the biggest prick in Lapland, come to pick you up. I ran over and the Colonel swept me up in his arms and spun me around and said, Let's go to the woods. I said, I'm in my work clothes, and he said, It doesn't matter, you'd be pretty even if you had your head shaved and your ass tarred. Alatalo, his chauffeur, drove us to Ivalojoki, where we ran into Major Paasonen, an army doctor who was there measuring the skulls of the Inari Lapps. There was a two-person canoe waiting for us on the shore. We packed up the food the Colonel'd brought, waved at Alatalo, and set out.

It was a wonderful, cool Lapland night and we daredeviled it up and down the rapids. I screamed when we hit the rough spots, but I trusted the Colonel completely, I was sure he knew how to keep us out of danger. We sped along like that for hours. I watched a hawk diving for fish. It got its claws on a whopper, and then the fish pulled the hawk into the river and drowned it. Around noon we found a nice little stretch of shore downstream. We steered the canoe there and got out. The damp leaves along the water were absolutely silent under our feet. We set up camp, built a lean-to, and made a little fire. The Colonel caught a monster trout along the shore with his bare hands and we roasted it over the flames. Long after midnight, as darkness slowly spread across the sky, we lay down to sleep. Early the next morning I woke up and saw six-pointed snowflakes drifting down onto the ashes of the campfire. The Colonel pressed me hard against him and whispered that he was afraid. I asked what he was afraid of. The blasted sky, he said. Have you gone nutty? I said, and he said, It's been staring at us so angrily for hours. I calmed him down and gave him a sip of moonshine and pretty soon he was gently stroking my cheek. I realized then how timid and paranoid he was inside. That seemed like a good thing to me. My father had been brave and timid in the same way.

Our trip lasted ten days. We paddled and ported the canoe across untouched tundra all the way to Ivalojoki. From there we looked out across the still, gray hills, the blue wilderness lakes with red boulders and yellow sands on their peaceful shores, and beyond them the southern slopes of Korvatunturi. Sometimes we were pummeled by hailstorms or drenched with sleet, but we just laughed. We lived on love, completely free from the shackles of the world. That whole trip the Colonel was like carrot soup, so soft and sweet that I fell head over heels in love with him all over again. We skimmed down rivers in our canoe and over the heavenly lake at Sevettijärvi, where the Kolt Lapps were learning to give up herding. They knew all the good and evil of the world because they'd been cast about hither and yon. There was such a thick bed of lichen in those woods that the Kolts' reindeer were twice the size of the Inari Lapps'. The Colonel sometimes went for a swim, and caught a fish every time he did. Sometimes a five-kilo pike, sometimes a fat perch.

We ended the trek at the Colonel's fishing cabin at Luusuanniemi. It was a mild summer evening, and I said I thought I'd take a swim. He said, Go ahead. When I got back he wasn't there. I called. Nothing. I started to get nervous, wondering if he'd gone out in the woods to look for kindling and had a heart attack. I shot off around the cabin calling his name. Finally I spotted him, lying curled up on a rock at the tip of the point. I ran over to him, afraid he was dead, but when I took hold of his shoulder I could tell he was alive. He curled up tighter and his face twisted like he was about to cry, although there weren't any tears in his eyes. I asked him what was wrong. After a while he managed to say that he was afraid of a war. I held his head in my lap and stroked his hair. When he had calmed down we walked back to the cabin holding hands.

He yearned for a new war, but at the same time he was afraid that if the Russians won and occupied little Finland, his head would be the first to roll. That was why he had those attacks, why he destroyed his papers and train tickets, old passports and photos of himself posing with Commander Göring at a forestry conference or holding a deer carcass somewhere in Germany. Then the feeling would quickly fade and he would once again believe in the all-powerful Third Reich and Hitler's thousand-year reign. He would get all excited and go on and on about how Finland and the Third Reich had a common enemy: cigar-smokers, by which he meant rich Jews, and cigarless ones, by which he meant poor Jews, plus Russkies and other trash. He believed that Stalin didn't understand anything about warfare, that the Russians were no match for us; they were subhumans who didn't even have proper guns to shoot with. But once the war began, he started to respect Stalin and called him a flexible leader. At the end of the war he said the Führer was a genius, but he didn't have any perspective, didn't know when to quit, while Stalin was able to lead in whatever way was appropriate to the situation, to change direction, to plan his course of attack.

Commander Wallenius, who the Colonel always called the Idiot General, asked us over for lunch on the eve of the Winter War. He was the Colonel's old comrade from back when the Lapuas abducted Ståhlberg, but he was also his greatest rival at every stage of the war. I'd been to Wallenius's house many times as the Colonel's girlfriend. It was always the same. First we ate and drank, then the Colonel and the Idiot General started fighting. Then we drank some more, and the combatants started to droop and eventually passed out. This time, during the first course of the meal, the Colonel pointed at me and said, This girl has the best pussy in Finland, and she knows what to do with it, because I taught her myself. Everybody at the table went quiet and I felt ashamed, but I was proud too. When we got to the main course the Colonel started talking about the coming war. Said that the Russians wouldn't attack, that they didn't have the proper equipment or weapons, or even winter clothes. That we would take them by surprise and beat them in a couple of weeks. Wallenius jumped in and said that wasn't how he saw it. He said he'd seen with his own eyes how well the Red Army was equipped, that there were hundreds of tanks and armored vehicles and bombers and other primo equipment on the border, and all their soldiers walking around with such grins on their faces that it made your hair stand on end and we ought to start thinking about whether we were ready to take it on the nose. He was trying to be a good friend and poke a stick of reality in the spokes of the Colonel's battle lust, but the Colonel just smiled and said the Reds were about to be salted like sardines. He said nothing could stop the war, and we were going to show Stalin who was sitting pretty. Wallenius was no man of peace, but he said that there were nearly two hundred million Russkies and less than four million of us. Coffee and sweet rolls were brought to the table. We sat silent. The Colonel was tapping his feet, he was so impatient for the war to start. He slurped down his coffee in one gulp and walked out and slammed the door. I followed him. I said, Let's go to the woods. He said, If you want to. I thought the plain, simple peace of the pine bogs would calm him down. But they didn't. We walked toward the village, holding hands. We stood quiet and wistful and looked at the beautiful forest where the Germans would later build an airfield for Rommel, and Rommel would never land. We got to the flat clearing at the edge of the village and walked over a damp, rotting shelf of land to where the open marsh was spread out in front of us. In that light I felt naturally strong and red-blooded and saw the sparkle of a thousand and one eyes around me. It was a sight that ought to have overflowed with beautiful, romantic ecstasy, but to him it seemed like the whole vast forest was the looming war, a fertile field, burned and ready to plant, sod for the harvest of battle. The woods didn't give him peace like they did me, and we quickly went home again.

After Katri died we had our first Christmas together. The Colonel gave me a lovely old diamond ring that had belonged to Katri. That meant we were officially engaged, and I was so happy. I was going to be a Colonel's wife and all. I thought that if I started having kids I could have my wedding that much quicker. I didn't, but the Colonel petted me morning and night and brought me perfume and carnations and chocolate by the sackful and licked my toes and sucked on the tips of my fingers.

When the Colonel teased me and hurt my feelings I took it hard and felt like the rottenest person in Lapland and the whole world seemed like a dark, gloomy place. And sometimes when I was laughing and happy he would do his best to wipe the smile off my face and put me back in the dumps. And then he'd start comforting me and make me laugh again.

I was in paradise. There was nary a woman as sublimely happy as I was in all the earth. Or in heaven, for all I knew. I waited for the Colonel's proposal, but it never came. I asked once, in a vulnerable moment, When are we gonna get married?

And he said tenderly, There's no rush.

The Colonel sealed my fate when I was four years old.

This is what became of me.

WE USED TO GO TO DINNER at the Pohjanhovi Hotel in Rovaniemi and sit so long into the evening that we didn't get home until the wee hours, when ashy gray light lay over the river. All sorts of people used to go there—during the Continuation War Generaloberst Dietl, our closest German friend, was there especially often, with his long, slender fingers so graceful as he smoked his gold-tipped German cigarettes.

Dietl once raised his glass and said that if it weren't for Sweden's mines and Finland's nickel the Third Reich's arms industry would be spinning its wheels. He talked about how ever since the First World War international fishing negotiations had been a cover for a nickel deal and we closed the deal later with the Third Reich. The one who used to talk the most about it was former commander in the czar's secret service—and Lapland chief of fisheries—Kaarlo Hillilä. As early as the summer of 1938 he was already saying that we were going to get an army together, and build a nickel mine at Kolosjoki and then go fight the Russkies. He used to talk about things that had happened twenty years before, when the Colonel and Wallenius'd had their own private war out in the woods in Karelia and Petsamo, fighting against Finnish Reds who'd fled across the border to escape the War of Liberation terror. The Colonel was already a big man back then and so was Wallenius, but Hillilä was just a pipsqueak who'd run away from home and wanted to be a soldier. He whined about how the Colonel and Wallenius had lured him and his little brother, Eino—just a couple of crazy, innocent kids—into this military outing of theirs. Eino never came back from that outing, and Hillilä resented the Colonel for it till the day he died. Naturally the Colonel thought going to Karelia had been the right decision, because he never made mistakes. After the war, in a moment of weakness, Hillilä once told me about a time they were in a little village in Viena Karelia. It was the middle of July, and him and the Colonel had been hiding near the edge of the village. Then an old man came walking down the road with a young woman following behind him, a strong young thing with sturdy legs and thick, heavy braids. The Colonel decided to stop them. He shouted "Halt" in Finnish, but the two of them just kept walking. So they ran after them. The girl had a broad face and sweet, dark-blue eyes. While Hillilä was talking to the man, the Colonel took the girl behind a woodpile, and a short time later he came back alone. So Hillilä asked where the girl was. She's over behind the woodpile, but there's not much left of her, the Colonel said. Hillilä was shocked, and he went to look. The girl was lying there raped and dead, with flies swarming around her.

When the time came for the Lapp provincial elections these two traumatized comrades were both running for governor—Kaarlo Hillilä, whose biggest idea was to make Greater Lapland a world fishing power, and the Colonel, who wanted to build up a Greater Finland, and Greater Germany. Even the Communists voted for Hillilä, because they thought the Colonel was unpredictable, a pig-headed man who always had to be right.

The Colonel was bitter about losing, of course, and wanted to get out of Lapland. And it just so happened that he got an invitation to a party Maila Talvio was throwing in Helsinki, so we popped down to the train station and bought tickets. The Colonel said, When we get to Helsinki, let's not go straight to the party. First I want to show you to my mother. I was thrilled to think my status had gotten high enough that he would take me to meet her.

The Colonel's mother, Desiree, was past ninety. She was a bent old burnt-out matchstick of a woman with a bald, bony head. She lived in a big stone house with gigantic pillars on either side of the entrance. *Välkomna*, she said as we came in. She'd had to learn Swedish as a girl when she worked as a housemaid for a wealthy family, so the Colonel was used to hearing it. It was sort of hard to imagine that this old bone-head going on about how rich and sophisticated she was had given birth to the Colonel.

We sat on a sofa in the parlor and a servant even older and sourer than Desiree came in carrying a tray of coffee and pastries with shaking hands. Please do have one of each, Desiree said. There were seven kinds, Swedish-style. The Colonel swigged down his coffee and disappeared into the library to browse the books.

So it was just me and Desiree. I was quiet. She looked me up and down and wrinkled her nose. She asked in a sarcastic tone who my people were. I told her my late father had been a comrade of the Colonel's in the Jaegers. She nodded her head a little and said wearily, *Vilken liten satan.* Such a little devil. I didn't know what to say to that. My father and the Colonel had actually known each other before they were in the Jaegers. They met at the turn of the century, at the Helsinki soccer club. That was back when Mom and Dad and my older sisters lived in Helsinki. I wasn't born yet. Dad and the Colonel were in the first group to go to northern Germany for Jaeger training in 1915, at a battle camp disguised as a scout camp. Dad was there for six weeks, but the Colonel stayed in Germany for four years. He volunteered for the Royal Jaeger Battalion's Twenty-Seventh Pioneer Company, along with Heikki Repo, who was later one of the Red Jaegers. When they weren't riding around Swabia in horse-drawn wagons they were fighting against their old schoolmate Marshal Mannerheim, who was in the czar's army back then. I was just three at the time, living with my mother and sisters in Rovaniemi in a cute little red cottage.

Desiree's chatter skipped around to different times and places. She was born in the backwoods of Häme and improved herself through hard work, a head for business, a sharp mind, and luck.

She started out as a maid for a Finland-Swedish family with a patriarch—an *underbart* man who gave her a little extra every month. And I had the good sense to hide those coins well away, she said. After a few years I went from maid to merchant. I was the hat and my late husband was the bonnet, so to speak. When Governor-General Bobrikov was assassinated I threw a big party, and the creme de la creme was there.

She ran a bustling butcher shop in the Eira neighborhood. The shop did well, and she used the money to expand her business. In her heyday she owned meat, milk, and import shops all over Helsinki, and a coffee shop too. She'd sold it all off except for the coffee shop, which she kept as security for her old age, and for the fun of it. She had used her profits to gradually buy up half the apartments in the handsomest building on Tehtaankatu. One flat for each of her kids. The Colonel had a five-room flat on the top floor that he'd been renting out ever since he left for Jaeger training. He'd never actually lived there himself.

We looked at photographs, although Desiree couldn't remember most of the posed, slightly faded people in them. But she remembered Einar. *Här är Einar*, she said, pointing to a little boy with her crooked, quivering finger. There was a black cross drawn on the picture. He died when he was three years old. *Här är Jakob.* There was a black cross on that one too. He died when he was five. She said that Einar had fallen down and hit his head on the edge of the table and died. Jakob, she told me, had been running after the cat with a knife in his hand and cut his own jugular vein open. He bled to death. The Colonel and his sister Maria had carried his little white coffin. I imagined the procession down the shadowed path to the family grave, followed by plodding, weeping mourners in black.

This is Johan, Rudolph's father, Desiree said, scratching at a bearded, bespectacled old face with her fingernail. And here's Impi, and Rauha. Then there were lots of pictures of the Colonel and his daughter, a little girl with a turned-up nose, and then pictures of the Colonel with the girl as a young woman. I pretended I didn't know who she was. Desiree looked around furtively. Then she leaned closer and whispered, That's Tea, the love child of my eldest, Maria, who lives in Sweden. I raised Tea like she was my own daughter.

Of course I had immediately recognized Tea, the Colonel's pet. She'd been a regular summer visitor at the border station ever since she was little. She and I were the same age. We used to play together. We even used to go to dances together. She came to visit later on, too, when we lived at the Villa, and spent the summers lazing about the house, but her visits were always poison to me. Whenever the Colonel came back from a trip to Germany he always had the best gifts for Tea and the second-best for me, even after we were secretly engaged.

The Colonel poked his head into the parlor. He had an executioner's gleam in his eye, and was holding a copy of Van de Velde's *Ideal Marriage*. Desiree's mumbling stopped like it was cut with a knife. I showed the Colonel his father's portrait and said they were like two berries. He didn't even glance at the photo album, just muttered, These lazybones nowadays expect the government to take care of them when they get old and helpless, but Father was cut from a different cloth. Got up at five every morning till he was eighty-nine to go birdwatching on the beach at Lauttasaari.

He sat down in an armchair and gave us a weary look. Desiree was pointing at a picture of the Colonel as a baby, lying naked on a lambskin. He was a greedy fetus, she whispered. So hungry for milk that he came out a month early and latched onto my teat like he was starving. She looked over at him and hissed into my ear that he could be sweet when he wanted to but all the family's flaws were concentrated in him. Then she rang a little bell that was on the table and the servant appeared in the doorway. Desiree ordered her to bring the sherry. We sat in silence. The servant returned with a bottle of sherry and two glasses. Desiree poured some into her coffee cup and immediately drank it down. She filled it again, and drank it. The third time she filled it half full. Then she cleared her throat, straightened up, and started talking again. She said she used to wrap the Colonel up tight in a swaddling blanket when he cried at night, and hang him from a hook on the side of the tiled stove while she was working during the day. It was a practical thing, you know, because the stove kept him warm, and it let his excretions run down. He would squall until he got tired and then fall into such a deep sleep that she'd have to splash cold water on his face like a christening to wake him up. She said he learned to talk when he was just nine months old, but he didn't walk until he was three. And he hadn't spent a single second in one place since. Every morning before going to work his father would tie his ankle to the foot of the sofa so he couldn't burn himself on the hot stove. Desiree got advice from a book that said to spank him with a switch every day when he'd done something wrong, or in case he did.

The Colonel gave Desiree a downright greasy look, then got up, clicked his heels, and walked out.

Desiree leaned closer and whispered, Poor child, you're just a silly kid. You don't know a thing about life. You may love the Colonel, but if you love yourself, if you love life and ain't interested in killing yourself, then don't ever marry him. Better to be engaged for the rest of your life.

I wondered about that and asked her what exactly she meant.

She let out a deep sigh and said that once a woman's married all she has to look forward to are days filled with endless sacrifice, and nights of painful, vulgar shenanigans.

I thought she just wanted to hold on to her son till the last. I told myself that his other women had been old or ugly or otherwise deficient, that they didn't know how to love him right. They didn't know how to make him happy, and that was why they all went early to their graves. I thought my unconditional love could wash away the bad in the Colonel and fill him with good. He and I were one. We were in it together—our steps, our breath, in time with each other. We had the same ways, the same values, the same rhythm of life. My love was so strong, so powerful, that I could cure him of his character defects, whatever they were. With the invincibility of youth I convinced myself that I could turn the Colonel's heart toward good. Desiree waved a hand toward the door and said, War's made a devil out of him. And you are not a pretty girl.

I curtsied and went out to the foyer, where the Colonel was waiting, and I looked at him with new eyes. I didn't see evil or ugliness. I saw a handsome officer. He had on his parade uniform and his shiny Prussian Army boots. I adored a man in uniform, loved the smell of leather, always asked him to put on his best outfit when he came over. And he almost always did, right up until we got married. Once we said the Amens he started showing up in filthy rags with the tops of his rubber boots all stretched out and hanging and would only put on his parade uniform when he was on important official business in Helsinki or, later on, when he was going to screw some other woman. Once during the Winter War when he was on his way to a secret meeting with General Siilasvuo—a man just as volatile as he was—he sent for General Wallenius's personal orderly to polish his boots. That boy stuck his arm in those boots up to his elbow and spread the polish so precisely, took his time with every little bit of those boots, used about ten different kinds of brushes and bits of cloth. I would've liked to have him there to shine the boots all the time.

We took a cab from Desiree's to Maila Talvio's place. She was Finland's most beautiful author, and had an international reputation because she had traveled all up and down Italy with the fascists. Maila was a personal friend of Mussolini. She was well known in cultural circles as a woman of many talents. She wrote books and was a gifted speaker. She was a political activist and a journalist for the Patriotic People's movement newspaper. She ran a finishing school and was a Friend of the Fatherland, and later, during the war, she and her artist friends founded a fascist party. Maila had such a wonderful husband, a professor. He once said that ordinary people are all stupid and any decisions about the country should be made by wise men amongst themselves. Maila, like all of us wise people, equated Germany with culture and philosophy and romanticism, and even Lutheranism.

She was one of those charming hostesses who had a lovely apartment decorated in the patriotic Karelian style where she threw lots of parties. There was always a program of cultural offerings at her parties, from Schubert to Bach, violin solos to folk dances, culminating in some inspiring speech followed by appreciative discussion. All through the 1930s the discussions were about the great countries planning to bring peace to the world, and about the riches of nature, and how to divide them up. Germany wanted to be a world power again, with interest, and us Finns wanted to be their sidekick and become the great power of the North.

Maila ran to the door to greet us. The Colonel kissed her hand and I curtsied. We all spoke German, in the Continental style. Maila introduced all the guests personally. There were ten of us. After the introductions there was a musical performance and then a speech from a representative of the Prussian Academy of Sciences. He said that the Third Reich, led by the Führer, would bring about a new birth of the German people, the creation of a new, shared culture, and that Germany had made a one-hundred-year leap forward in human development.

In point of fact, the Führer had banned everything European

culture was best known for: democracy, liberal ideas, scientific thought, intelligence. He replaced it with metaphysics and mysticism, the myth of racial science and the worship of the Aryan race. The man from the Academy of Sciences said Germany was a happy, well-run country now. The Germans did their work, took care of their homes, ate well, had a little free time to unwind, went to marches on Sundays, and were looking forward to having considerably more living space. He finished by unveiling the Führer's new animal protection law, the most strictly enforced in the world, and his measures to neutralize antisocial elements, namely, Reds and other filth. He said the conservatives of the world were too careful, they didn't want to do anything new or uncertain, but the titans of industry in Germany and America had given the Führer trainloads of money, and the entire German middle class supported the ideology of National Socialism.

General Buschenhagen was at the party, looking on while the other guests talked. After the Colonel died, our driver Alatalo told me that a few years later, in the spring of '41, Buschenhagen had come to Rovaniemi and Alatalo had driven him and the Colonel from the airfield to the hotel and on the way Buschenhagen had told the Colonel that the Gestapo, with the approval of the Finnish Ministry of the Interior, had ordered that the Lapp civilian government be replaced by a wartime government, in other words, put under military leadership. And the Colonel said, That would make the Germans an occupying force. And a long silence fell over the car. Then the Colonel said that there were so many Reds in Lapland that he couldn't take that risk right on the brink of another war. And they went back and forth about it all the way to Ounasjoki Bridge, and they decided that they would let Kaarlo Hillilä, who was a National Socialist, run the civilian government, for the sake of appearances. It was a wise decision. They had Lapp Bolsheviks fighting the Russians side by side with German Nazis, and they kept things going smoothly as long as they could. A week after they made this wise decision, the Rovaniemi airfield was already full of German fighter planes. Finland deployed all its available troops, and Hillilä took on the official German title of Landespräsident. He said it had to be an impressive title so the German officers would show him respect, but nobody could be bothered to use such a fancy word and they all just called him the Emperor.

There were a few Finnish heavyweights among the guests at Maila's house, the same faces that were at all the parties. Probably the most important guest was Veikko Antero Koskenniemi, a professor from Turku University who had toured Hitler's Germany and Mussolini's Italy with great admiration. He was a Latin scholar, Europe's leading expert on Catullus, the court poet of the White faction who'd saved Finland from the Reds, beloved author of the words to *Finlandia*, and later, with Goebbels's blessing, vice-chairman of the European Writers Union. During the speech by the man from the Prussian Academy of Sciences, Professor Koskenniemi clapped enthusiastically and interjected shouts of Heil Hitler and sometimes even Ave Caesar. Koskenniemi was a great man, greater than his times. It grieved him how the Communists were trying to politicize the arts. He had a lot of power because he sat on the boards of dozens of foundations and publishing houses and generally got his two cents in on all cultural matters. He had a wife and six young mistresses, just like Catullus.

The poet Heikki Asunta was there, too, a wreck of a man weighed down by money troubles, who was fond of saying, We Nazis love aesthetics. According to Asunta, we represented real Finnishness, we weren't like those racially weak Marxists, with their cosmopolitan orientation, taking orders from their Red Pope in Moscow. Later in the evening Asunta gave a speech where he criticized the use of Swedish language in the schools and universities, bad-mouthed Finland-Swedish cultural imperialism and

Bolshevism, and said that rich Swedish speakers controlled Finnish industry and commerce, always coughing up money for their own kind instead of sharing it with the Fatherland. He finished by talking about how our identity was in our common language, the one official language, and our task was to unite the whole country to build up Finnishness. We don't need translated literature, he said. Asphalt literature from the city. We believe in the idyllic life of the folk, country people with common sense and good ideas. The Colonel didn't clap. He was of a different opinion when it came to Swedish, but he wisely kept his mouth shut.

Maila had seated me next to the author and poet Iris Uurto, who sat in a thick cloud of perfume with her purse clutched tightly under her arm. Iris was keenly interested in the human body and how Nazi ideology had commandeered human instinct, intuition, emotion, and sexuality for its own purposes, when they rightly belonged to the individual. Iris didn't like the Nazis at all. I have no idea who invited her there. On my other side was the philosopher Alfred Rosenberg, a Jew who was the Nazis' number one ideologist after Hitler. He loved brave little Finland and its people. He thought they were spiritually wholesome, pure and unspoiled, a perfect example of Nordic cooperation. He told me he'd taken his philosophy from Schopenhauer's passive spiritual life, Nietzsche's *Übermensch*, and Goethe's noble and practical quest for harmony and rationality. He said that being born is our greatest tragedy.

That made us all stop and think. Then we raised our glasses for another toast. The war was still some way off, but we were already burning to begin. We knew the war was coming, but nobody knew when.

My father made me a daughter of the White Guard. The Colonel made me a Nazi.

And I'm not ashamed of either one.

I WAS LISTENING TO THE RADIO, and it occurred to me that the more German martial songs they played, the closer the war was getting.

First they cranked up the distrust and hate for the Russians little by little, calling Stalin a mad dog, talking about the Great Bear threatening the little Maiden Finland and how pretty soon they'd be taking our territory. At that point we were all buzzing, full of ourselves, bragging about how Finland was going to be a great power in three months flat. Even peace-loving men were ready to fight. The lamb shoving itself in the wolf's mouth, as President Paasikivi put it afterwards.

In the spring of '39 the Colonel went to the beach at Hanko with some SS officers, and when he got back he said, They'll strike up "Life in the Trenches" now.

They didn't, not yet. And not over the summer.

It was our last autumn of peace and I was playing solitaire in the office at the Inari border station when the Colonel came marching up bristling with excitement. I felt pretty tickled and proud to think that this big scary man would come all the way to Inari just because he missed me. He stood on the porch and shouted, Little poetess, we're going to Poland. And I said, Have you gone nutty? There's a war going on down there. He said he wasn't nutty; he was a professional Finnish soldier and we were going to the Eastern Front to see how the Germans handled supply transports in occupied areas, and some other things, so we'd know how to do it right once we had occupied Russian territory all the way to the Urals and put our ancestral homelands back on Finland's map. He'd heard that the Führer was emptying out Warsaw and everybody who lived there was being taken to work camps all over

Poland and now the Germans were going to move in and take their place and Warsaw was going to be a German city. He'd been ordered to go there as quick as he could, and he'd got permission to take his secretary with him.

We boarded an unmarked Finnish military plane and it flew us and a couple of German officers in civilian clothes across Lapland, semi-incognito. There was also a German on the plane who was wearing a Finnish Army uniform and spoke Finnish fluently. He greeted me cheerfully and stuck his arm up in the air. We took off early in the morning, first flying over East Karelia to survey the situation. There were men in the fields swinging their scythes, and babushkas washing white clothes on the river stones. The Colonel, who wasn't easily deceived when it came to military matters, smiled and said it looked like a cinch, but one of the Germans, who had already exchanged his worn suit for an SS uniform and adjusted his cap with its little skull and shiny silver cord on his head just so, looked down his nose and said that on the contrary what we were seeing below was a sign of proud self-sufficiency and confidence of power. The Colonel laughed and said in Finnish, These Germans don't know a thing about Russia.

I saw firsthand on that trip that there was a machine already in motion, and it was about to roll over more than just Poland. All the young men were handsome heaps of muscle. You don't get a body like that from morning calisthenics and making peace. I saw troops commandeering sports fields, cannon platforms in city squares, tanks in industrial areas, and other signs of preparation for war. And of course fleets of fighter planes.

As we soared over Europe, I wondered how my uncle Matti was doing. Would he pick up a gun and fight the Russians when the war started, or would he run across the border to Leningrad, even though he knew that Stalin had executed his old comrades?

The plane made a stop in Berlin. We passed a week in the

Savoy Hotel, where Greta Garbo once stayed, while we waited for Himmler's office to grant us passports and entry permits to the occupied areas. You couldn't just go there; entry was highly restricted. We ate smoked eel and pork butt in fancy restaurants, swigged down muscat wine, strolled up and down the streets. We saw people loitering in front of half-darkened cafés, a Jew tied to a streetlamp for people to spit on, shop windows filled with evening gowns made of silk, macramé, and Bergamo velvet, women with half-filled shopping bags standing in line at a place that sold feather boas, streetlights swinging from cables, crowded trams, wet asphalt gleaming like a misty summer lake, tenements that blossomed from the black earth, dirty streets, factories and courtyard passageways where we made love in the dark. We went for a nighttime walk in a park on Kantstrasse. The solitary moon drifted across muddy puddles and flashed over the shining sides of oil drums stacked on piles of folded tank tracks. There were so many city lights that they illuminated the very sky and gave the night a gray glow. Every evening we took a walk around a pond in a park called Lietzensee, enjoying the peace of the great city. Soldiers in uniform patrolled the park, their pants pockets bulging with grenades. There were corporals and sergeants and SS men milling around who always shoved their caps back on their heads before asking the soldiers for their passports and travel passes. The Colonel said the Germans were all awfully ugly, but that was a lie, if you ask me. I bought beautiful clothes, which the Colonel paid for: a satin skirt and a matching blouse with a frilly collar, black and flesh-colored silk stockings and lacy underwear. The Colonel plied me with egg liqueur and Hildebrand chocolates, the kind that when I put it in my mouth made me feel like a better version of myself.

We got permission to go to Poland, to a city that was Lviv in Polish and Lemberg in German. Before we left we both had to sign a pledge of secrecy. It said that we couldn't tell anyone about anything we saw there, and if we did we would be exterminated. We flew in a small, single-engine plane through black rain and blood-red fog. We were driven through the city, and everywhere I looked, in shop courtyards, in front of office buildings, in city squares, on boulevards, at beer halls, were young men in uniform. Some held machine guns, but others, drinking in front of cafés, left their rifles leaning against the wall.

Himmler's office had arranged to let us stay at a place that had been taken from a Jewish family, a Biedermeier manor house nestled in among oak trees. The facade of the main building had lots of tall, multipaned windows with fancy plaster moldings. The foyer had a marble floor and a vaulted ceiling painted with pink clouds on a blue background and shepherd boys with their sheep, all bordered by plaster cornices patterned like acanthus leaves. The parlor had Corinthian columns and pilasters with huge, dark-colored pots between them. The new owner of the mansion was a thin, very mild-mannered SS captain name Gunther. He owned a chain of glove shops in Munich. His secretary was one of those crisp Nazi girls who always wore a black skirt and the simple, elegant blouse of the Nazi youth. It had a tie, which she wore cinched tight. Her and Gunther's wife, Ilse, got along swimmingly. Ilse was a slow-moving woman with a broad face, but she had a rose satin dress that fit her well. And pretty ankles. She liked to count money at the kitchen table and talk about how much the Catholic church had helped the Third Reich in building and development. In addition to those three people there was a kid whose lips twitched and a lot of servants. Wretched, skittish Jewish prisoners, or whatever they called them, were constantly tending the fertile lands of the manor—fields, gardens, flower beds, milk cows, and pastures of sheep. I watched out the window every morning as about thirty women prisoners were brought in to tend the vegetable garden. Their heads were shaved and they were all wearing paper-thin barn coats. They were followed by two older, uniformed SS guards leading a handsome, well-fed rottweiler on a leash. One day it was raining hard, like it was sprayed from a hose. The north wind was blowing and the weather was so harsh that we stayed indoors all day. I looked out the window and there were those same women, stooped over the vegetables in all that rain. I didn't see the guards, but the rottweiler was there guarding them.

I made friends with Ilse. She told me how wonderful it was to live in the new Greater Germany, where there was such unfettered freedom and Germans could do whatever they wanted to do. She showed me two handsome paintings and some gold jewelry that she had rescued from the apartment of a professor who had disappeared and a set of porcelain dishes from another apartment, and a mink coat and fur stole from another. It seemed nasty to me to take other people's things without their permission. My father taught me that it's a sin. But I kept my mouth shut, since I was a guest, and they were taking such good care of us. Dad taught me that when you're in another country, you do things the way they do them. But I cried to the Colonel at night and said it was wrong to steal. It's not stealing, it's confiscating, he said, and besides, they don't need those things anymore anyway because they're gone. They're dead, sweetheart.

I saw a lot of things there that horrified me at first, like hanged bodies swinging from tree limbs, but by the time I'd been there a week I was used to them. The more Ilse told me about life in the East, the more I wanted to know about it. I asked her one question after another, and she told me, showed me, instructed me. She told me she was a "brown nurse" and a member of the Nazi Party, and she had lots of duties. She sent Polish boys and girls off to heaven and injected poison into seriously wounded German soldiers to release them from their suffering and let them rest on the right side of God. That job had a lovely name: euthanasia.

Ilse was always coming and going. She had a fire under her ass to sacrifice everything for the good of the Third Reich. I came to realize that the Führer had given German women an awful lot of responsibilities. Besides all the things I mentioned, Ilse was also in a women's police unit that kept guard at market squares and distributed rationed goods. And there were millions of German women like her, tied to these sorts of jobs, official duties, work organizations. Everything was organized beautifully, down to the last detail.

A while after our German trip, the Colonel came into the Inari border station like a thundercloud one day and yelled, Ready to go? I said I was. Alatalo drove us to the west coast through fields of fat ears of barley. The Colonel said we were going to Pello, where Yrjö von Grönhagen, a special adviser to Himmler, would be waiting for us, and that Himmler'd given an order to let him take pictures of all the hilltops where the top French scientists and astronomers had gone to figure out whether the earth was a pumpernickel or a berliner. The Korteniemi manor house was the fanciest house in Pello, and we were going there. But I wasn't feeling my best. There was a buzzing in my head and my arms and legs felt heavy. I didn't mention it to the Colonel, of course, just tried to be cheerful and lively. Von Grönhagen came out to meet us as we drove up. The hostess had set a long table. There were porcelain dishes and a silver coffee service, and there was grouse and well-aged rabbit in mushroom sauce to eat. Everything was rich and delicious. For dessert we had cloudberries and cream and hot coffee. After dinner I felt horribly sick and ran to the privy to throw up. I chucked up my supper and a lot of bile too. The Colonel shouted that it was time to hit the road. I staggered out of the privy and said I wasn't up to it. He gave me a long look and said, Your face is downright green. Why don't you stay here. The lady of the house can take care of you, and we're only going for a week. I stumbled into the house and the hostess let me lie down on a bed in a guest room. A very tidy room with clean bedding. They put a chamber pot and a basin at the foot of the bed. I lay quiet. It burned when I peed, and my brain was boiling and my face was melting. I sweat right through the quilt. The lady of the house gave me a clean nightgown and dry sheets. Then I got an awful chill and shivered so hard the bed shook, and pretty soon the whole room, and I was crawling across a frozen lake, about to die, with a herd of horses all around me. Then the fever hit me again and I got the sweats and now I was crawling through a dry field in southern Germany and everything was blood red—rocks and tree trunks and dried-up flowers and grass. I wandered in my sickness like this for several days. When I started to come to, the daughter of the house was sitting by my bed. She looked like she had only half a head, and she had a horrible, thick mustache, like Stalin. She was singing from an old Zion hymnal. She looked red to me, too, and so did the light on the ceiling, and the windowframe. A week later I was recovered and chatting with the granny, who was more than a hundred years old but still had a memory as sharp as a razor. She told me her grandmother was fathered by a Frenchman, but still, she had her wits about her.

One night about three a.m. the Colonel walked into my room, screwed me, and said that von Grönhagen had finished taking pictures of the views from all the highest hills and they were going home the next day. Alatalo would be there soon and they could take me to Inari, then him and von Grönhagen would continue on toward Rovaniemi and the war.

October came and I lay awake at night. I watched through the border station window as fluffy snowflakes floated through the black sky onto the gray, snow-covered fields. I thought of the Colonel's gentle touch, his strong hands, his sharp, perceptive mind, and his ungovernable body. Intelligence was his biggest gift, but it muddled his head too. Around the end of October, there was such a big boom from east of the border that a geranium fell off the windowsill, and I thought, It's starting.

But it wasn't, not yet.

The lack of sleep added up, but I was full of energy in the daytime. I chopped wood, shoveled snow, paced back and forth in the office, and knit socks and rifle covers for unknown soldiers. And just when I couldn't wait a minute longer, the Colonel called. He was in a bad mood. He griped about Marshal Mannerheim and the president and how they'd started sucking up as soon as the real war got going, just when we were ready to kick the Russians' ass. He said he knew that Stalin had proposed an exchange just the week before—You give me the land east of Leningrad and I'll give you three times as much land in the North, and the marshal and the president had agreed to it, but luckily at the last minute Eljas Erkko, the foreign minister, happened to have his wits about him and put the brakes on the deal. Stalin liked to keep Erkko hopping.

Pretty soon it was November and a big wind came up and shook the woods and struck up big waves on the lake and everybody knew that the Red Army bagpipes were about to break into "Katyuska."

Then one day the sky froze and the big German guns started to boom in the icy, sulfur sunlight. They were spitting whole dragons straight at the sky while men with M27s cleaned up what they could see on the horizon. A siren wailed from a tower. It was the kind of siren that comes on with the turn of a crank. I ran outside and the whole road was ringing, the stunted trees were howling, the sleet-battered woods were wailing for mercy. Then the noise suddenly stopped and a silence fell like none I've ever heard before or since. It felt like the breath of the whole universe had been squeezed into a vacuum-sealed coffee can. I stood in the middle of the road like a pillar of salt, with no hat or gloves, wearing my rubber boots and a sweater wrapped around my neck. Then there was an explosion. I could feel it in the soles of my feet. There was a burst of powdered snow, tree branches flew off, and mud and blackened stones pattered on the ground. Then I heard an all-clear bell from the direction of the church. I looked at my feet to see if they were still there. They were. A Russian bomb had hit the milking barn at Kuttura crossroads. I made my way back into the office through the thick silence. I wasn't panting, wasn't in shock. I felt strong, ready to sacrifice myself if that was what it came to. There were burned trees along the road, limbless trunks, soot raining down until the snow was black.

The Colonel's car came speeding into the yard so fast the fenders rattled. He came rumbling in the door all worked up and full of excitement and whispered in my ear that Daddy was off to war, and if I was good he would bring me back a matrushka or a Rublev icon as a souvenir. My cooch started quivering and we took off our clothes and laid down on the soft bearskin in front of the fire and watched as the flames melted each stick of wood to ashes one by one. I thought about the summer before at Tenojoki, when we sat on a mossy boulder shaded by old spruce trees and the Colonel said that no one in this world had toenails as sweet and slender as mine.

The Winter War was going full bore. Chugging like a steam engine. Jaeger General Wallenius announced that he wasn't going to shave his beard or wipe his ass until the Russians were clobbered— and you can't kill a Russian without shooting at him. The field chaplain said, Don't joke about death. Death is life's greatest accomplishment. The men of Lapland were put on a train, caps slapped on their heads. Some boys ended up in Hyrynsalmi, some in Salla. They were bringing the dead into Inari church less than two weeks later. Me and another girl were there to meet them. The company chaplain was running around with his arms flapping, there was such a rush to bless the bodies so the martyrs could get on the bus to heaven. They found boys in the frozen mud who'd survived the front, their bodies crawling with fleas and lice and scabies and worms. A fresh batch of soldiers stood miserable around the graves, staring at their own fate. They pointed their rifles at the winter sky and fired a salute and we made crosses out of birch branches from the spring pruning.

I didn't see the Colonel once in all of December and January. He was commander of a special battalion deployed in various places on the front and I was left at the border station to fend for myself. I was filled with an empty feeling. I couldn't see anything in life. Just sadness. My love for him became a nightmare. I couldn't eat or sleep or anything. The nights were the worst. Loneliness would slosh around inside me and I'd get a terrible pain in my cooch, my back, right below my heart. Sobbing out my pain and despair into the mute night. The lack of sleep eventually hit me so hard I could hardly get out of bed. Every time somebody came into the office I thought it was the Colonel. Every time I saw somebody coming down the road, they looked like the Colonel. I sat by the phone for days waiting for him to call. If I thought about doing the laundry, a second later I was thinking about the Colonel. His face was the one thing on my mind, his voice, his hoarse laugh, seemed to come from every direction. I was clearly slipping over the edge of sanity. I was a tattered scrap of bottomless love, and I would've wasted away if Pastor Pulpakko hadn't happened to come by. He saw the shape I was in and he knew how fragile and slippery life can be and he started feeding me, first with tiny spoonfuls of oatmeal and the medicine of the heavenly word. He washed my hair with fresh birch sap, rubbed honey on my chapped lips, filled my mouth with

Hildebrand chocolates, and I started to perk up. He said later that I would've been a juicy catch for him, and for his Word of Peace movement, but he was merciful and didn't impose his holiness on me. He ended up in the Karelian Isthmus toward the end of the Continuation War. The realities of the front lines crushed his faith. He gave up his position and spent the rest of his life working as a custodian at the school by the river.

I had seen with my own eyes how a person could change in three hours from a common ne'er-do-well to a proper soldier, how quickly a free young man could be made part of a herd. Erkki Olthuis, who was working for the military police on the front, brought the youngest Mattus boy into the border station one day. The kid had been out in the hills looking after the reindeer and had no idea there was a war on. He wasn't a deserter, but he was more than half a notch in that direction. Erkki had a rifle in his hand and he even had it cocked and jammed into the kid's ass. He said, We've come here so this dodger can change into some field grays. It's forty below outside. And the boy took off his Lapp clothes and put on a Finnish army uniform. Everything was where it should be except that he didn't have a belt. I went to the closet and got him the Colonel's leather belt from Germany. It had a fine buckle, engraved with the words *Meine Ehre heißt Treue*, My Glory Is My Loyalty. He slipped it into his belt loops, hooked both hands on the buckle, and gave me a wink. My button sat right up, and I was so shocked at myself that I could hear my own heart pumping and feel it all the way to my toes.

Then one night when I was sitting in the easy chair the phone started jangling. It's me, the master of boondocks warfare and your beloved, the Colonel said. I miss you so bad I've started licking tree trunks. I was so relieved and happy he was alive that I burst into tears. Just hearing his voice filled me with life, and all my misery was wiped away.

After that the hard-frozen days zipped right by. I warmed up the stove, played solitaire, and pined away over romance novels. One day I was leafing through some hack's pulp romance and I thought, I could write one of these. And I started writing romance stories in secret, just for fun. When I was writing the time would fly by, morning turning to night and me still sitting there. I'd flip through a magazine or look at my old photo album or my scrapbook where I'd pasted pictures of my favorite movie stars and I'd pick out characters that looked right to me and I'd make up a past for them, and a present, and sometimes a future too. Then I'd pick up a pen and a completely different story would come out of me onto the paper, with different characters and everything. Writing is like real life—you can't control it. I've never shown those stories to anybody.

In the last month of the war the Colonel managed to get leave to come home two more times, as a sort of combat bonus. The first time, on short notice, he came in wearing clean battle grays, his boots polished, with a jolly look on his face, and swept me up in his arms and said, Suffering has made you more beautiful. I guess it suits you. I stuck out my tongue. The second time was for a whole twenty-four hours, and he took me out into the light of the full moon, out onto the road that led to the woods. There was a smell of frozen swamp. Big snowflakes sifted down from the sky onto my nose, onto the fierce, churning riverbank and the thick branches beyond the fields covered in crusted snow. Safe from an evil world, we marveled at the polestar and the Colonel said it shone brighter than a grenade blast.

One Sunday when the Winter War was over and the Continuation War hadn't yet started I was relaxing outside, flipping through a German magazine, and I heard the Colonel yell for me. I jumped up out of my sunning chair and ran inside. He was holding something behind his back, and I heard a meow. He'd brought me a cat, which I named Nefertiti, because she was so proud and full of herself. The Colonel said that another war was about to begin. You're going to be on your own again, with nobody to keep you safe and comfort you. This kitty can give you some tenderness and hope in tough times.

He took off my clothes and carried me to the bedroom. While we were at it Nefertiti came in with a fat mouse in her mouth. She stopped in front of the easy chair and started throwing the mouse in the air and catching it and batting at it with her paws. Drops of blood were dripping out of the mouse's mouth and it was trying to get away, but she kept snatching it up again with her sharp claws and biting at it. The mouse was screeching something awful, but still kept trying to escape. Its little nose was clenched in terror, laying there on its side. Death was getting its grip on the little thing very slowly but surely. Nefertiti swatted at it, trying to get it to move again. The mouse trembled in a terror of death, batting its paws, and the cat listened to it whimpering and suffering. Its tiny feet groped at the air. Nefertiti thought for a moment that it was dead, but when she clamped her teeth on its throat she realized it was still alive. The mouse went silent and heavy, but still struggling to breathe, to the very last, difficult breath. Finally its strength gave out. Death moved through its body, sliced through its thin tether to life, and eternity flew out of it, and it didn't move anymore. Its body went stiff, its little feet were chilled with death. Nefertiti watched in a sorrowful trance, her head bent over the departed creature, then she turned her back on it and started licking her fur. She patted out a sleeping place with her paws and slipped into a contented nap. The Colonel made love to me gently and deeply. Afterwards he said, God doesn't feed the lazy, and he left to get ready for the war.

I got a ride from one of the German border station guards into

Inari, a place that's dear to me, where the trees can't really grow and the tundra moths eat every leaf from the birch trees. I surrendered myself to the motions of nature, and keeping the books at the border post. The white, nightless night of the North took good care of me. The chill August land was always in motion. The wind carried the scent of new-mown hay and clover and tarred boats to me on my silent walks through the trees on the shore of Lake Inari. I saw the shining, dark silver leaves of shrubby willows, was soothed by the rustle of dry brush, the autumn storms that could blow up in minutes, the islands, the great expanse of the lake.

That was the summer before the war really got going, with Finland fighting alongside its German comrades in arms.

I saw it all at Ilse's house—the camps, the violence, the killing, the murder, the liquidations. The hate. I knew. And so did everyone else in Finland.

If you knew how to read, you knew what the Nazis were doing.

I WAS AT THE ROVANIEMI RAILWAY STATION when the Germans arrived in 1940. They were greeted with even more excitement than the ones who came to Oulu in 1918. I stood on the steps next to the Colonel with my chest out, wearing the Tuusula folk costume, and Hillilä and General Wallenius stood to the right of us. It was a foggy day, but the sky was bright over the green woods and marching music was playing, making the birches curtsy to the rhythm and the pine trees roar, This is it. The first person off the train was Generaloberst Dietl, a thin man in a tight-fitting uniform. He walked straight up to the Colonel. The Colonel clicked his heels, straightened his back, stuck his arm up in the air, and said Sieg Heil. Dietl did the same. Then they smiled sweetly at each other like they were old friends from the Colonel's Germany days. Wallenius had a sour look on his face—Dietl should've greeted him first, since he was a general. I shook the Generaloberst's hand, too, and his bright-cheeked orderly gave me a big bunch of flowers. That smell that only German men have was wafting from the train. They all had well-cut uniforms and shiny boots. There was Maurice the MP, from Flensburg; Klaus, a sergeant who'd been chancellor of the technical school in Greifswald; Helmut, a corporal and shop assistant from Frankfurt; and many others.

We welcomed the officers and other leaders. The prettiest girls in Rovaniemi handed them bouquets, and after a series of elaborate welcoming rituals the soldiers carried out rabbits, parrots, polecats and guinea pigs, dogs and asses and horses on leads that they took behind the station for some fresh grass to nibble on. The Alps Jaegers put up tents, laid their rucksacks and ammo bags out in neat rows, glancing at us now and then with their heads cocked, their songs ringing in harmony all the rest of the late-summer day.

Once the tents were up they built their field kitchens. Soon enough, big steaming cooking pots were sending the aroma of goulash wafting out over the lake and the moss-covered ground. Me and Rebekka sat a ways off, because we were grown women, and snuck sidelong glances at them. Some of the teenage girls were nearly drunk with their presence. One of the soldiers shouted, Come have some stew, girls! And they said, No we won't. Why? We're scared. Of what? Of you. Why? You'll poke us with your ski poles—you're a bunch of mean, uncouth Nazi pricks! No we're not. We wouldn't hurt a fly. Then the girls laughed and ran over to them, like all the yelling was just a game. I and Rebekka, who had blackened her eyebrows with charcoal, followed them just to make sure nobody kicked over a kettle of fish. The Alps Jaegers offered us some of the stew with lots of meat in it, and gave us drinks of cherry juice from their own canteens. To us poor girls it all tasted so good we nearly burst into tears.

When they'd filled us up we went to sit by the fire. I had a nice chat with a boy named Ervin, who had a belt buckle that looked familiar. It had honor swords and the words *Meine Ehre heißt Treue*. I asked him what it meant, pretending I didn't know. He said it meant he was loyal to the Führer, the German people, the father-land, his division, and his comrades in battle, and that he believed in German victory. The older soldiers started setting up the artillery. They pondered a long time about where to put the guns, until a long-range patrolman named Herbert looked out at the mowed field of the nearest farm and said, How about over there? And it wasn't long before you could hear the salvos as they started practicing their shooting.

The people in Rovaniemi were treated to marvelous parades and marches just about every day. At the end of a parade the Germans would let loose great quantities of colored balloons and the kids would run after them. Those Germans could charm any small, pure, and innocent heart.

A sweet-faced German staff sergeant named Fritz who'd been a teacher at an agricultural college in Bavaria ran a canteen at the edge of Rovaniemi market square, and Rebekka fell in love with his lips. She said they were sensual. He had sad green eyes and a lively look about his face. Naturally, Rebekka wanted to marry him and move to Germany after the war, but it wasn't possible. Fritz said that the wife of an SS man had to have blond hair and be at least 160 centimeters tall. Rebekka was brunette and two centimeters too short.

I got into Fritz's canteen on Rebekka's coattails and got all kinds of treats. There was pineapple served in champagne glasses, Leipzig-style food from the kitchen, and wine from Naumberg. Every time I went there Fritz would leap to his feet, put his fists on his hips, tuck his chin into his collar, and say in a cute little voice, Heil Hitler! I thought it was so funny. The Rovaniemi Reds who hadn't been executed in 1918, and their snot-nosed offspring, went around bad-mouthing the Germans and cursing at them, out of jealousy. But they did it in whispers so the Germans wouldn't hear them.

Once when I was shopping with Rebekka at Fritz's canteen two of the SS MPs came in. Fritz clicked his heels together and whipped his arm up straight. One of them asked him for his identification. He dug in his pocket for it, and I could tell he was really nervous. His face went white. The MP glanced at his papers and said, *Jetzt gehen wir*. Like a lot of our German friends, Fritz fell into a black hole. The new canteen keeper was an SS boy from West Prussia with only one star on his collar.

When the Germans came the Colonel wanted to have a big party at his timber castle at the border station. He rubbed his hands together and said, You're going to find out what a wonderful hostess you can be. You're going to set a table so handsome that even the Germans will see there are a few people at this latitude who know how to live up to Aryan standards.

The Colonel's castle, once presided over by Katri, now by me, was a simple, rectangular building. The main house had six rooms and a kitchen downstairs and four rooms upstairs. It had a birch-lined drive and a root cellar with smoked hams hanging from the ceiling. The Colonel made sure there were always pots of clabber on the shelves with a thick yellow crust on them. Tyyne Petäjäinen, the chair of the youth workers celebration committee, baked bread for the Colonel every week, which we stored in the cellar in a faded old wooden box. I can still smell that yeasty bread, it was so good. The Colonel liked the simple life. As far as architecture went, a plain dugout and a field cot suited him best. Albert Speer's baroque monstrosities made him laugh.

I christened the party A Patriotic Evening, and most of the real work was done by some Lottas from Rovaniemi.

The guests started arriving before noon. The first was the Colonel's good friend Vidkun Quisling, who was Norway's Nazi leader and a terribly cultured person. Then came General Siilasvuo, a drinker. That was before the Colonel hated him. Then there were the Colonel's Bavarian friends, Heinrich Reitz and Wilhelm Laqua, who were both majors in the Gestapo. They brought me a tall flower vase made in East Prussia. Major Laqua made a toast and said that the quickest link between Germany and Finland now was through Kirkkoniemi, in the strip of Norway between Finland and Russia. He said the Winter War had been a disappointment, it was true, lackluster because it was too brief, but that was behind us. We had a common enemy, and many common interests, and that was all we needed. The Colonel gave a speech too. He said that in the heart of every Finn was a fear and hatred and contempt for the Russians, an aversion that'd been in our blood ever since the Russian invasion of 1714. And that went for the Jews, too, because Russianness plus know-how plus big business was basically Bolshevism. Then we raised our glasses many times to this idea of our common enemy.

The German National Socialist Party had an office in Helsinki, and Wilhelm Jahre, commander of the Finnish division, arrived with a few scoutmasters, who were more or less equivalent to the Hitler Youth. There was also Yrjö von Grönhagen, without his camera this time. He was a pretty man, an anthropologist who did research for the SS Ahnenerbe Institute and was a close friend of Himmler. After the war he spent his winters in Greece and his summers on the banks of the Tana River running a travelers' hostel where the Colonel and I spent many pleasant evenings in his elegant company. The Finnish State Police were represented by Tauno Heliara, who praised the Führer as the greatest political leader in the history of the world, and poor Paavo Säippä from the State Police, who was a pragmatist.

During the Winter War there was an episode with Paavo when he came into the office in Inari one day and said he had a burning issue to discuss with the Colonel. The Colonel was snoring in the back room, and we went and woke him up. Paavo and General Wallenius had just been to Berlin as guests of the Gestapo to beg for Germany's help. None was promised. Paavo and the Colonel sat at the desk for a long time poring over taped-together pieces of map. Then we had some coffee and in subdued tones Paavo gave us the news from Berlin: Himmler had said that the Finns were an inferior race, shiftless, slow, clumsy, stubby people who ought to be sent to live on the surface of the moon along with the Jews. He said Germany had a secret agreement that they would give Finland to Russia and get Poland and the whole Baltic for themselves in return. The Colonel said, Who cares about Poland and the Baltic?

And Paavo said that just when he and Wallenius were getting ready to leave in shock, Wallenius whirled around and told Himmler, You've sold us to Stalin just like Judas sold Jesus, and you'll reap the consequences.

Paavo wiped the sweat from his brow and a long, grim silence fell over the room. Finally the Colonel broke it. He sighed and said, No cause for alarm. No time for panic. The Nonaggression Pact between Stalin and Hitler was just something Germany cooked up to throw Stalin off, to give Germany time to prepare for an incursion into Russia. Paavo was quiet. Pacts are made to be broken, the Colonel said, lighting his pipe, like he always did when his nerves were starting to get to him. And he was right about that. Just like he always was. Paavo Säippä wasn't a fanatical Nazi. He was a more moderate, international man who couldn't really hate the Communists, maybe because he liked them as people. That was why he got fired from the State Police after the Winter War and was replaced by the Colonel's friend Arno Anthoni, who was just about the staunchest Nazi on the Finnish peninsula.

Feminine beauty was represented at our party by Rovaniemi's youngest Lottas and the wives and marriageable daughters of bank managers and other notable citizens. They flocked around the men, smiling coyly or openly, whichever suited them. We all had a rousing good time. Somebody played some Chopin on the piano, somebody else sang a short song, and of course we read Koskenniemi's poems in German and recited the Kalevala in Finnish.

The spurs of the Third Reich were jangling as pretty-faced German officers on surveillance duty sauntered around and made chitchat in the parlor and the smoking room. They smelled like eau de cologne. Their chins were smooth and their hair neatly slicked. The guest of honor was the general and nobleman Nikolaus von Falkenhorst. The Führer had declared him an expert on all things northern and put him in charge of everything that happened up here. He was stationed at Kirkkoniemi, but he often dropped in as far south as Rovaniemi. This expert in arctic conditions didn't know how to ski or sauna, and he hated white nights and reindeer. His dick was covered in scars—he'd either got a grenade in his lap or some whore'd taken revenge on him. Falkenhorst, like most Germans, liked strict military discipline, so he was always under a lot of stress, his face all screwed up, so tense and nervous with his own troops that he was as gray as a head cheese, but he used to go hiking with us out in the backwoods or out to the islands to drink beer, and he would dig out his camera and lie on a boulder snapping pictures of ptarmigans or foxes or what have you. He sweet-talked the Colonel, told him how much he loved every little creature that God created, like ants and inchworms and Tasmanian devils, said he had the biggest beetle collection in Germany. He told jokes, sang old German folk songs about farting dogs, even got up and danced sometimes. He was so romantic, such a dreamer full of childish enthusiasms, that it was hard to believe he was the same man who'd struck fear into the hearts of men on both sides of every border. Sometimes he brought Hungarian pear schnapps with him, and we lapped it up. Once, in a fit of sentimentality, he confessed that his greatest dream was to end his life on the stage, performing *Rigoletto* at the Nuremberg Opera. He'd been a friend to Finland during the War of Liberation, and was always flattering us. He said the Finns were unbeatable as athletes and soldiers and Finland had been an outpost of resistance to Bolshevism from time immemorial. He explained to me, with one of those red-and-blue teacher's pencils, how the official colors of the Third Reich expressed the content of their ideology. Red stood for National Socialism, white for the purity of the nation, and black for the rest. He didn't explain the rest—the racial persecution, the killing of the sick and deviant, the glorification of violence and cruelty, the reduction of women to machines, the use of slave girls, the people starved to exhaustion, the death camps, the master race morality, the fanatical enthusiasm for health, the worship of spartanism. Most of all, like other Germans, he was silent about the fact that the Nazi leadership couldn't stand Christianity, while us Finns had always been devout Lutherans.

Our Patriotic Evening ended when it was time for the Colonel to go back to the war. He was in an awful hurry to get to the front before they ran out of Russians. I wished I could go to the combat zone too. This was in June of '41. The men were trying to broaden the hips of the Maiden Finland, and us women's job was making sure the men could concentrate on the fighting. The Colonel vowed that he wouldn't laugh until the Finnish flag was flying over Viipuri again. I thought life on the front would be a lot more fun than playing around with my ledgers. Out there, anything could happen. The Colonel was against me going, of course. He said he wanted to keep me safe in the wilds of Lapland like a treasure frozen in amber, that he was haunted by the idea of all the pussy-hungry men on the front lusting after me, that I might slacken my chastity and give some handsome young officer an opening. He said, You're my girl and I don't want any other man to look at you. He said the two of us had something special together, different from everybody else. In the end I agreed with him. I didn't want to turn fat and ugly like Vanni Luukkonen, the Lotta leader. I contented myself with organizing a sewing circle at the Pohjanhovi Hotel. We spent the Continuation War there gabbing and sipping sherry and now and then sewing lampshades with string made from the dried skins of some creature, following a pattern out of one of Ilse's German handicraft magazines. The light-colored hide made a beige thread, the darker kind made tan. It was just like the reindeer sinew thread the Lapps use for sewing fur coats and harnesses.

Rovaniemi was the big city of Lapland during the war—it still is, just like Helsinki is for the South—and the Pohjanhovi Hotel was the heart of Rovaniemi. During the Winter War there had been about forty newspaper men from all over the world living there. During the Continuation War there were some six thousand German soldiers quartered in town, and only about eight thousand of us civilians.

Wallenius, the hero of the Winter War, was the brightest star of Lapland in his own opinion, and he had his nose in everything. He posed for foreign photographers with tears in his eyes, patting the curly head of a Russian prisoner, and it probably ended up as a centerfold in *Time* magazine, although he actually treated all the prisoners like shit. The Colonel was jealous, of course. He would've liked to be the center of attention. He always had to settle for second fiddle and it was torture for an ambitious, competitive man like him. But Wallenius just surpassed him; it was as simple as that.

Once during the Continuation War I was skiing through Rovaniemi in a hard frost past the airfield the Germans had built, the one named after Rommel, smelling the sweet aroma carried on the wind from the big bakery in Little Berlin, when I saw a man in a beret standing in a snowdrift. I asked him what was wrong. He said he was lost. He was a Frenchman, a poet and journalist for *Le Monde* named Bernard le Cor. I admired him immediately when I noticed his kind, playful eyes and the sympathetic way he had about him. I put my skis under my arm and led him back to the Pohjanhovi. He invited me to supper. I accepted. We had goose in jelly and salmon à la Kalsta, and finished up with a jam cream, which was vanilla ice cream with jam mixed in. He talked with me about how European values and cultural heritage have restraints and prohibitions to keep unscrupulous people from realizing their basest desires and most selfish wishes. We became close friends.

Bernard wrote me a poem called "War's Bloody Tedium." Then

I wrote him a tender verse about the happiness I'd left behind in the ruins of my own home in the Far North, and when I read it out loud to him I burst into tears. Pretty soon we had a heap of poetry. There's one bit Bernard wrote that I remember: *The Germans win only summer wars, they cannot prevail in the winter, they even attacked France on the 5th of May, to be sure that the rains would be over.* That's my own rough translation. The French version had a better cadence to it.

He was right about the Germans. They make a big fuss about how enchanting the wilderness is, but they're afraid of the woods, afraid of mist and fog and silence, cloudy skies, hollows, fields and bogs, lakes and ponds, beetles and mosquitoes, bears and reindeer and blackflies.

It was at the Pohjanhovi that I met an Englishman named Jack who was a con artist and a thief. He said he'd come to fight against the Finns. Jack was an illiterate adventurer. I wasn't the only one he charmed; there were a couple of camp followers of ill repute who cried after him for months. I also got to know Magnus Dyrssen, a commander in the Swedish-Norwegian volunteer army. We practiced reading aloud on the banks of the Ounasjoki. I read Goethe to him in German and he read Strindberg in Swedish. He was a very sharp-witted, deep-thinking man. And good-natured. We used to sigh over how people nowadays had become adding machines. I would've introduced him to the Colonel, but a Russian sharpshooter picked him off before I had a chance.

In Rovaniemi we got all kinds of gifts from the Germans. Generaloberst Dietl wanted to keep up his skiing skills like an Alps Jaeger should, so he ordered the German troops to scrape off a spot on the side of the ridge at Ounasvaara and put in a slalom course. It was actually a gift from Dietl to the Colonel, who was the founder of the local ski club. The Colonel was an expert skier, of course, because he'd been required to learn it as part of his Jaeger training.

He probably even could've beaten Dietl. The Germans taught me to ski too. We were on the slopes several days a week, enjoying life. Those soldiers were carefree kids. The high-ranking officers made all the decisions and bore all the responsibility, and all they had to do was follow orders. Once a soldier had finished his work for the day—like teaching me to ski—he would rush off to play cards or go carousing. The Colonel had some of that kind of soldier in him too. Him and Dietl used to sit in the sauna for hours, sometimes until morning, and the Colonel's nephew, Rudolf, if he was around, served as their steam ladler, back washer, birch-whisk cutter, and toenail clipper. They liked to humiliate him. I had to rescue him once when Dietl and the Colonel were making him run around the sauna naked, throwing cold water on him in below-zero weather. He might've died of exposure. Rudolf ran away to Germany later on. He joined the Finnish Waffen-SS and served for two years. Fought in Ukraine, and came back a broken man at the age of forty-three. But Dietl was wonderful company in other ways—witty, funny, and smart. He loved fried reindeer and Austrian vinegar sausage. He brought us some, and it was tasty with aquavit or a glass of wine. Whenever they were toasting to Finland, Dietl would say in perfect Finnish, Down with the Russians! And the Colonel always answered, To Greater Finland and Free Karelia! I thought Dietl was Austrian, but after the war I found out he was actually from Bavaria. At the opening ceremony for the ski slope Dietl told me, You're the prettiest woman in town.

That was just six months before his horrible plane crash.

The war basically just intensified the feelings the Colonel and I had for each other and deepened our bond of shared experience. The nearness of death was like a magnet. I've never felt so alive as I did then. Surrounded by the ruckus of the war, the fun side of his personality shone brighter. His grasp of events was amazing, and he could put things so sharply that it sometimes cracked me up. He knew how to charm a smart, pretty young woman, and his knowledge of the world was remarkable. He knew all about history, geography, chemistry, psychology, even philosophy. He had a sharp eye that I never tired of. He knew how to behave in such a way that it never occurred to me to think, He's awfully old. Except sometimes, of course.

Revenge was in the zeitgeist. They called it the Nationalist Cause. They built a military operation to prepare for it. Sweden helped the Third Reich by providing money, mineral ore, and ball bearings. The Führer put it all into the war industry. Himmler dropped in on Rovaniemi and informed Dietl that he wanted to take a real Finnish sauna. Dietl went looking for the Colonel in a panic. Could Himmler come to your house? You have the best steam in all of Lapland. That was fine with the Colonel, so Himmler and his press attaché, Hans Metzger—a real Nazi and a bosom buddy of Risto Ryti, the president of Finland at the time—came over to our house. Metzger entertained us with his impressions of Helsinki slang. He was all smiles. Called us "honorary Aryans." We ate, drank, and headed to the sauna. In addition to the men there was me and a few other perky-breasted young girls. We tossed off our clothes and squeezed in on the bench together. Then the men came in, and last of all Himmler, still in his long johns, with his glasses on his nose. Everybody thought that was odd, but nobody said anything. He praised the steam and used the birchwhisk on us girls with great relish. Every so often we went out to the anteroom for a drink, then back into the steam. When it was time to wash we all soaped each other's backs, but nobody dared to touch Himmler. He didn't bathe at all because he was afraid his long johns would get wet.

The good times ended in December of 1941 when Marshal Mannerheim refused to send Finnish troops in to capture his beloved Leningrad. Of course the Colonel was awfully disappointed.

He said it was obvious that the Baron—he always called Mannerheim the Baron—was no military leader because he didn't know a thing about how to make war and was completely behind the times. He said that Mannerheim was a shithead and there wasn't a single Finnish general who was going to put up with such a decision and that General Airo had to follow him around with a mop, cleaning up his messes. The Colonel knew that if him and the Germans had been in charge of Leningrad, they wouldn't've let the people out. They'd've left them there to die over the winter, and in the spring German sanitation crews would've come and cleared away a million Russian bodies. But they didn't take Leningrad, so the troops on both sides of the border had to dig in and build trenches in the woods. The Colonel said it'd been the Baron's dream since 1918 to be promoted to commander of the czar's army and the White Guards in Russia, but that didn't happen so he had to settle for this trivial post as leader of his own country.

The horrible, exhausting trench warfare lasted two and a half years before we got back to normal fighting. The helpless waiting took a toll on the Colonel's nerves. He couldn't stand staying put, bellowed about how that bleeder's foot-dragging would kill even a strong man, how the boys were jerking off till their spines melted, how he'd spent enough time in the trenches on the Misa River and it hadn't done them any good. He didn't actually go to the trenches himself, of course, or practically even see one for the entire war.

In my memory that was a tough time, but also fun. The Colonel was tense and waiting like a crazy man for the fighting to start again, but we had a good time together. He was able to stay at my place in Inari for weeks at a stretch. He took me out to the woods and we listened to the ptarmigans and capercaillies and he took my hand in his and whispered, I love you, I love you, I love you, and my heart was like a shooting star that lit up all of Lapland. I thought nobody could love anybody like I loved him and my love would never fade, never change as the years went by, never turn into a lukewarm fondness the way it did for everyone else. My love was more fiery than that. My passion was my religion, and I was ready to pray and suffer for it. I lived for the Colonel, and I would've died for him if that was what he wanted. I catered to his every wish and enjoyed serving him. I was such a whore for him that I never thought of myself or my own desires. I made myself be just what he wanted me to be.

I'd say the high point of the war was in the summer of 1942. That was when Mannerheim had his seventy-fifth birthday. The Colonel got two invitations to the celebration, and he knew that one of them was for me. For weeks there were whispers that there might be a special surprise guest at the party. We flew straight from Rovaniemi to Ilmola in a German plane. I looked out the window and saw places below where enormous piles of logs were burning, flames leaping into the air, the land black with smoke.

There were a lot of guests at the party. President Ryti was there. He said that the Führer certainly was a warm person, a cordial, benevolent man, a great personality. The defense minister was there with his humorless wife, and Bishop Tapaninen and General Talvela, who didn't like Generaloberst Dietl at all. But the high-light of the evening was when the Führer himself arrived. He was traveling and had stopped off in Finland to stretch his legs and get a couple of extra shots of Eukodal in the ass from his personal physician and snort a noseful of cocaine and chew on a piece of pine sap rolled in salt to make his mouth taste normal. When he walked into the party it gave us quite a start. He was a stunted thing, with a round belly like a baby and a throbbing vein on his right temple. The Colonel looked like a young man next to him, although they were born the same year. The Führer was wearing a khaki-colored uniform with an Iron Cross and a gold National Socialist medal, and under it a snow-white shirt with a large collar and a pretty necktie, tightly knotted. He had a thin diagonal strap across his coat and a thick belt. With one shaky hand he held on to his belt and with the other he brushed his hair off his forehead. I looked for those world-famous ice-blue eyes. I'd heard them called sad eyes, too, and lonely. But I didn't find them. Didn't find that famous stare, either, supposedly black and bottomless. His eyes were bleary and cloudy. And cold. I stood off to one side and I could see the famous skin of the Führer. It was wrinkled and peeling. He had pimples all around his nose. And his nose was all pitted like it was made out of Bakelite.

Marshal Mannerheim, who by the way never would eat good Finnish pike but enjoyed a bit of roasted crow, glared at the Führer from across the room, looking like he'd swallowed a hand grenade. The Colonel said later that Mannerheim was in a bad mood because he knew Germany was losing the war and it irked him to share his party with a loser. The Führer swaggered and chuckled and made the mistake of slapping the Marshal on the back. The Marshal did not like to be touched at all. Of course he didn't, growing up in a big old manor house with a gaggle of syrupy women pawing at him.

I ended up with war duties, too, and the longer the war went on, the more work they dumped on me. The pace kept accelerating and the orders changed all the time. Sometimes it felt like I was losing my mind wondering when it would end.

At the peak there were twenty-nine prison camps in Inari where they locked up Russians who'd surrendered or been captured. Most of the camps were run by the Waffen-SS, and my job, since I knew German, was to keep an account of the number who died, were shot, or escaped. The Germans paid the Finnish and Sami a bounty in liquor and tobacco for every escaped Russki they caught. One Russian was hung from a pine tree and left dangling there, another one was shot and left lying in a snowdrift, one was chased to a hole in the ice and drowned, and another one was tied naked to a tree with barbed wire for the mosquitoes to eat alive. Bolsheviks, commissars, *politrouks*, and partisans got off easier. They were shot on the spot. The enemy soldiers suffered more in the war than their officers did.

I was responsible for keeping track of the camps run by the Finns too—one in Ivalo, one in Palkisoja, plus prisoner-of-war camp number 9 at Ajos Harbor in Kemi, the regional camps in Rovaniemi, Kemijärvi, and Sodankylä, camp 19 in Oulu, camp 21 in Liminka, number 4 in Pelso, and the one on Jäämerentie. Jäämerentie is the road from Rovaniemi to Liinahamari. There were eight more camps on that road. I also kept the records of the bodies for Stalag 309, a combination work camp, prisoner-of-war camp, and concentration camp that had branches at Alakurtti, Vuolajärvi, Rovajärvi, Korijärvi, Kairala, Nurmi, Lampela, Seipäjärvi, and Rovaniemi.

One day in December I was penning tidy columns of numbers in my ledger and adding them all neatly up when the Colonel called and said, Decorate the tree and clean the house, I'm coming over with a German guest. They didn't arrive till after ten. The Colonel opened the door and in walked the Führer's architect and minister of armaments, Albert Speer. My heart did a somersault and my legs felt wobbly. Speer was limping badly on his right foot and looked like he was in a lot of pain, although he tried to smile at me. Hulta offered him a cloudberry aperitif and he slugged it back in one go. I invited him to sit down to dinner. He had no appetite, although Hulta had made a delicious reindeer roast. The Colonel ate and Speer complained about his leg. I told him we could call for the Colonel's doctor, but Speer said no. He was awfully nervous, sweating and pacing up and down the room. The Colonel got an unopened bottle of French cognac from the cupboard and they drank half of it. Speer finally relaxed then enough to talk about what was troubling him. He had a blood clot in his leg, and he had heard that the Führer had ordered him killed, so he'd escaped in a private plane to Rovaniemi before the killers could get to him. He twisted up his arms and his face and burst out crying. The Colonel slipped out to the foyer and made a call to Little Berlin and told them, Come take this traitor away. Pretty soon there was a knock at the door and some Germans in civilian clothes came in and grabbed Speer. His face went colorless, and he didn't say a word.

In January of 1943 I received an order from the Colonel's superiors to go to the Kuolajärvi concentration camp and conduct an inventory. There was something off in the records and they wanted me to add up the numbers again. I called the Colonel and told him I was being sent to Kuolajärvi. He said he wouldn't let me go there alone. I landed in Rovaniemi and had to wait for him there for a week. We flew to Salla in a German military plane, then were driven to the airfield by Generaloberst Dietl's scarface Bavarian driver, who was sloshed and drove like a maniac on the hard-frozen road. I was screaming and the Colonel was laughing his snorting laugh. Then an awful snowstorm blew in. From the car I saw a flock of young women in ski pants outside the barracks mess with handsome German soldiers buzzing around them. I envied them a little.

When our plane landed at the airfield near Suulajärvi, a sad sight met me. Finnish boys in proper winter gear and half-naked Russian prisoners were shoveling the landing strip in that terrible, freezing storm. Every time a gust of wind tossed a drift onto the strip they had to shovel it off again. Alatalo drove us to the concentration camp. It was ringed by a pair of barbed wire fences two and a half meters high, and between the fences were sharp stakes, wires, and an alarm system made out of tin cans. There was one commander, two lower-ranking officers, and forty-eight soldiers guarding the place. Outside the barbed wire was a mound of sand covered in snow, and on top was a sign that said, Here lie a hundred short-necked Russkies. Quite a few of the half-starved prisoners had bloody diarrhea running out of their pants and onto the snow to freeze there. I was really deeply shocked, because I'd never seen anything like that in Finland before. I had seen it in Germany, but that didn't count. I'd already forgotten about it. And I hadn't yet lived through everything that happened toward the end of the war. I wasn't disillusioned with it all like I would be later. In a fit of pity I offered one of the prisoners my gloves, and then the head of the camp said if I gave them to him he would court-martial me. He said giving supplies to the enemy was treason. The Colonel stepped between us and slapped his right hand down onto his holster, then he took his pistol out and aimed it at the man and scowled and said, Didn't anybody teach you how to run a camp for these subhumans? In Germany you'd be hanged by your balls from the nearest oak tree for such a disorderly operation, but since we're in Finland, I'll just order five hundred lashes.

That was just the Colonel being sarcastic, which the camp commander understood. All that evening whenever no one was looking, and in the backseat on the way home to Rovaniemi, the Colonel kept taking me in his arms and holding me so tight I couldn't breathe. At one point he told Alatalo to stop the car and we made love on top of a tank barrier, between the slabs of concrete and twists of barbed wire.

Toward the end of the Continuation War there was awful confusion in Inari. The place was swarming with German Alps Jaegers who couldn't fight anymore. They'd lost their nerve. They were afraid of the Russian partisans. All the signs were saying that the end of the war—the peace—wasn't going to be pleasant. The

atmosphere just sort of started to dry up and all the most important German leaders started to disappear one by one. We were on
our own again.

The summer of '44 was the hardest. That's when a plane crash
took our beloved Dietl away. He had been to visit the Wolf's Den—
that's what they called the Führer's headquarters—and on the way
back his plane crashed into a mountain in the Alps. Many others
had died the same way, like the architect who was Hitler's favorite before Speer. He'd been to visit the Wolf's Den, too, and also
crashed in the Alps on the way back.

Dietl's death was a heavy blow to me. The Colonel consoled
me, said that Dietl had known his fate, and he'd left behind a beautiful farewell before he boarded the plane in Rovaniemi. I thought
for many years that Dietl never would've allowed the Germans to
lose Lapland, but the truth was that he'd planned out how they
would burn Lapland to the ground on their way out.

That same summer, the Colonel and me and Falkenhorst were
in the timber castle sitting around the table, drinking coffee cut
with cognac. All of a sudden Falkenhorst started coughing. The
Colonel was really startled and thought he might be having a heart
attack. Falkenhorst grabbed his head with both hands and in a
faint little voice he said he felt so horrible thinking about how
when Germany won the war he would have to send his dear friend
and his beautiful lady—in other words me and the Colonel—to a
gas chamber. He said the racial doctrine of the Third Reich taught
that the Finns weren't Scandinavians, we were Magyars, like the
Hungarians, and we'd be exterminated immediately, or have our
eyes poked out and get sent over the Urals as slave labor for the
Siberian mines. He said he felt sorry for us because he was so fond
of us, and he felt sorry for Finland because the Finnish people
had given their all to advance the cause of the Third Reich, never
knowing that their dogged work for the Führer's victory would

be their own downfall. Me and the Colonel went quiet. We didn't know what to say. I just said I was going to get some more coffee, walked away, and went in the kitchen. The whole next week the Colonel's face was off somehow. A feeling of doom spread to every cell in my body.

The Karelian Isthmus was lost, and then came the Red Army incursions, and the Gordian knot started to come undone. A defensive victory, in spite of Mannerheim. In actuality, we lost, and called it a victory. The forced peace dawned, the war in the East was over, and the Moscow Armistice was signed. It was an armistice and not a peace treaty because Stalin wanted some time to think about what he might like to add to the list of demands he'd stuck onto the Moscow Peace Treaty in 1940, before the recommencement of hostilities. In the end he didn't add anything. He decided to follow the czar's example and take pity on the Maiden Finland as a special case, a nation in a class of its own. He thought, Let's reward those Finnish boys for putting up a good fight. After the war, people would appreciate that gesture. But the war wasn't over yet. We still had another war ahead of us when the Russians demanded that we drive our friends, the two hundred thousand German soldiers in Lapland, out of the country. I was listening to the radio and Olavi Virta came on singing "Siks oon mä suruinen," which is just about the saddest song in the world, and by the last note I was sobbing. The telephone rang, and it was the Colonel. I could hear in his voice that something consequential had happened. General Siilasvuo, the hero of Raate Road, who'd been transferred to a desk job after the disaster at Kiestinki, was sent back into combat and launched a rear attack against the Germans, on Marshal Mannerheim's orders—or actually Defense Minister Walden's. I've been superseded! the Colonel shouted into the phone. All these turncoats and traitorous dogs coming and going as they please all around me and keeping secrets from me.

They're about to hang me from the nearest tree, I know they are. I said, That can't be true. You're the ranking liaison officer. Not anymore, apparently, the Colonel yelled. These pricks need somebody to discipline them. I'm going to talk to Generaloberst Rendulic.

The next day the Generaloberst invited the Colonel and me to dinner in Nampa village, about fifty kilometers north of Rovaniemi. German headquarters had been relocated there a few weeks earlier.

A car with commander's flags and an SS license plate with runish lettering came to pick us up. When we arrived I saw right away that the Generaloberst, who usually had the cockiness of a sharpshooter, looked depressed. We were told to sit down on the sofa and an orderly served us dry martinis. The room was quiet. I didn't know what to say, although I didn't usually have any trouble talking to him. Finns and Germans have similar styles of talking—we both take praise and criticism very seriously. Finally I asked Rendulic outright what was on his mind. There was a long, heavy silence, and he said that it was the thick Finnish forests and not being able to see the open sky through the tangle of trees that was making him gloomy and anxious. I told him that when you go farther north the trees end. Then the men started peering at a map and wondering about the hotshot general Siilasvuo's rear attack. There were all sorts of opinions going around about it. People said Mannerheim must be ill, or that the Germans had killed him, or the Russians had replaced him with a double. They couldn't believe he would order his troops to attack their own German brothers. Rendulic and the Colonel stood side by side poring over the Finnish and German maps. Both maps were marked with German withdrawal timelines. The Colonel told me later that the German maps looked completely different from ours.

Rendulic turned to the Colonel and asked if he would consider transferring, serving in the SS. A servant brought in a Wehrmacht uniform and a contract to sign. There was a long silence, and then

Rendulic said, We're planning to establish a Finnish commando regiment to fight beside the Germans against the Russians and Finns, and the Führer hopes you'll accept the command of this regiment. The orderly opened a box lying on a side table. It was full of crisp Finnish currency. Another long silence. I swallowed. I couldn't look at the Colonel's face.

Generaloberst, the Colonel said, I love Germany, but at the moment I have only one fatherland, and it is Finland. I'm sure you understand.

After this we enjoyed a good cup of coffee and some cognac, and the car drove us away again. That's how I've always told the story, but the truth is a little different. The Colonel never said, I have only one fatherland, and it is Finland. He yelled at the top of his lungs, You satan Nazi pigs! Now you offer me a general's stripes? Just to embellish my suicide? Now that you're already out of the game, because you've lost it completely? You didn't offer me anything when you were sure you were winning except the guillotine or a punch in the face. You call us Finns subhumans, mongoloids with stunted craniums, and offer us reserved seating in your gas chambers when you're winning. Go ahead and use our treaties to wipe your ass, but do it carefully, because pretty soon every last one of you is going to hang. I'm not going to kill myself. I still have some self-respect.

And of course we didn't drink any coffee. The Colonel marched out with his heart turned pure gray and gave a lazy shove to Chief of Staff Hölter, who lowered his hand to his holster and might have pulled out his pistol if Rendulic hadn't gestured for him to let it go. The same sleek car was waiting outside to drive us home to Rovaniemi. On the way we saw a company of German infantry marching toward the northeast. Five men from the company were crawling along at the edge of the road, and they bleated when they saw our car. I said, Look at that. The Colonel said, They're on all fours to show us that they're lambs being sent to slaughter up north.

When we got home we knew we had a tough war against the Germans ahead. The Colonel didn't want to take up arms against them, so we had to go underground.

We packed our most important possessions into two suitcases and told the housekeeper Hulta to take good care of the place, and Alatalo drove us toward the South, and exile.

We didn't witness the German withdrawal, but Hulta did. She told us that one morning the Rovaniemi church bells started to ring and the train engines blew their whistles like it was Judgment Day. Hulta went running to the railway station. Our German brothers in arms were there, scrambling to get on the transport train however they could. Every rail was filled with long, black cattle cars. Parrots screeched, rabbits were eaten, hamsters and polecats disappeared, donkeys were slaughtered, dogs yapped, and some horses tied at the end of the station shuffled their feet as artillery was rolled onto the cars. It took several days to load the trains. The tents and field kitchens were taken down and packed away, the trains whistled their departure, and the cars, festooned in dry rowan branches, jerked into motion and disappeared into the forest.

Then it was the German foot soldiers' turn to leave. As they marched away to the North, they set fire to every headland and hollow and string of islands, and threw grenades into barns and sheep sheds and chicken coops. The Colonel's border command station was a goner too. Hulta had time to save the floor vase that Laqua had given me and a cream pitcher that once belonged to a Jewish professor in the Warsaw ghetto. A while later they burned down my office in Inari. No great loss, but the new Alps Jaegers didn't know Lapland or its prominent people and they burned down the

Colonel's beloved fishing cabin out in Luusuniemi too. He never forgave them for that.

The Lapland War, the burning villages, and Rovaniemi were left behind as we sped away with Alatalo at the wheel, headed for the fall colors of Kemi. The Colonel held my hand tight and said we would get married as soon as we got there. But I don't even have a wedding dress, I said. And he said, You're so pretty you don't need a wedding dress. Are we going to kill ourselves then, like the Führer recommended? I asked. Yes, we are, the Colonel said. I can't live in a world where National Socialism doesn't prevail. I'll shoot you first, and then myself. I can't rely on you to do it.

I was willing to die, if that was what he wanted. For me, it had nothing to do with Germany's defeat. A double suicide was proof of our great love. I just thought, We lost the war, and now we'll take whatever the Colonel thinks the next step should be. A lot of men died on the front before they'd even turned eighteen. I was already forty. I was ready to go if that was what my beloved wanted. I had no will of my own. My soul was still four years old. I'd never grown up mentally. Somewhere around Tornio the Colonel changed his mind about suicide. Let's see what happens, he said. But remember, I don't want to leave any children in this world. I heard myself say I didn't believe in them either. The Colonel said that military careers are for men without kids, the kind of men who aren't accustomed to tenderness. He said that there's no sense wasting money on a wife, that you ought to beat them instead. It made them kinder and more affectionate. I was startled, but in the next moment I was already telling myself that he was talking about the reality of the war that had grown up around us and almost trampled the beautiful words of love we had spoken to each other. I thought his words would soon turn sweet again. The war would fade into the background and a new life force and passion to build would take hold in him and in all of us.

Alatalo drove us through Kemi. The streets were filled with trucks with discharged soldiers huddled in the back under tarps. There were soldiers on bicycles, in horse carts, on foot. Nervous gangs of veterans flocked at bus stops, bar entrances, and shop fronts. They didn't know what to do or where to go. Trains clattered back and forth. The whole country was in motion. Along the highway we passed more soldiers—skinny, unshaven, silent boys, numb and weary and crestfallen, their eyes fixed straight ahead. Boys who were still just kids with no combat experience being hauled north by truck to the Lapland War, to be fed to the guns and have their lives drained away to nothingness. I started to feel disgusted by the war, but for a long time I kept it to myself. Boys fight with bare fists, and powerful men fight, too, but they do it with war machines. In wartime, soldiers are heroes. Their officers promise them everything while the war is happening, but then the war ends, and they get nothing. They're left to sink or swim on their own.

We were married by a field chaplain named Schiller who'd been with the SS and was an old friend of the Colonel's from the Great War. The Colonel was in a clean combat uniform, his boots shining. I wore a plain black pleated skirt and a black jersey pullover. It was like I was in mourning—but black was the formal color back then. We didn't have any rings, so we didn't exchange them. Alatalo was the only witness. There were no guests. After the ceremony, Schiller said that Roosevelt and Stalin were going to share the ruins of Europe between them.

We continued our trip. I felt childishly shy, but happy. After more than ten years together, we were finally married, and I was a Colonel's wife.

It was the prettiest, brightest, happiest day of my life to that point.

I once asked the Colonel why he tortured me,

why hardly a month went by that he didn't try to outright kill me. He said,

You always hit the ones you love.

WE MADE OUR WAY DOWN the disfigured body of the Maiden Finland and arrived in Tammisaari. As Alatalo drove us up to the large manor house, the Colonel said, This is our new home. From the outside it looked like a ramshackle place. Alatalo carried our suitcases to the half-rotted veranda, waved good-bye, and got in the car to head back to Rovaniemi. The Colonel opened the door and the inside of the house was as lovely as a fairy tale. We took our clothes off straightaway and ran from room to room looking for a bed. Ever since I was a kid I'd believed that hopes and wishes made the world go round, that we could live for the rest of our lives happy, believing in each other.

The house was an old mansion built between a pond and the sea. An industrialist the Colonel knew had given it to him to use as long as the political situation demanded it. The pond was called Lappi Pond, of course. The place had ten elegantly decorated rooms: a parlor with Biedermeier furniture, empire wall lamps, and real French lace curtains the color of ivory, a dining room with a massive, multibranched crystal chandelier, and a wonderful glassed-in veranda where we held crayfish feasts every fall for the next several years. There was a sweet lattice trellis on the front of the veranda with fragrant climbing honeysuckle and white acacia just like at Ilse's house on Germany's Eastern Front. From the dining room window you could see a big garden with old maples and lindens and fruit trees and farther off the endless, lead-gray autumn sea. Our time at Tammisaari made me a yard and garden person. I still love hazels and horse chestnuts and wandering in the stiff reeds and cattails along the shore and other wonderful things like that. Anything that rustles in the autumn wind.

❖ ❖ ❖

The first two weeks after we said our vows were a perfect time. I wandered from room to room like I was under the spell of some drug. Whenever the withdrawal symptoms from the war being over got too oppressive I'd pop a chocolate in my mouth. All my dreams and hopes and beliefs about life were at the height of summer inside me, and whenever I remembered the war I tried to keep all the best moments and adventures at the top of my mind. The Colonel got a cover job in Hanko. He was frustrated and depressed and grumbled about the paperwork, but he looked at me with pride and admiration. Now you're mine alone, and I can do what I want with you, my little poetess, he whispered. Your pussy is as soft and tasty as a young potato, and every evening it will hold me in its gentle embrace.

We built a sanctuary together. I was the soul of our home. I flipped through magazines, walked in the woods, and kept myself beautiful and desirable.

One evening the Colonel came home from Hanko as usual, and we started rolling around like we always did. I didn't notice anything out of the ordinary. He looked at me tenderly and whispered sweet things in my ear. Then I smelled a strange woman's perfume in the hair on his chest. I gave it a good sniff, and his eyes turned cold. He jumped up with an angry look on his face and snarled, What kind of whorish brassiere is that? I said, It's the one you got me in Berlin. He roared, Shut your hole, and he ripped it off me and yelled that no wife of his was going to walk around in slutty lingerie and he slapped me right in the face so hard that blood flew out of my mouth and nose onto the white sheet.

The first blow was followed by another. I could see the anger flooding up inside him. He was like a frenzied animal that turns on its hunter. I couldn't bear to look at him. He shouted in my ear that no bitch was going to chain him up and lead him around and keep guard on him like an animal, and he grabbed the torn brassiere off the floor and stuffed it in my mouth. His eyes shone with a hate as clear as ice, and with a sweet, gooey pleasure. His tight-closed mouth, the movements of his hands, the shape of his fists, the drops of sweat on his forehead, the fast pulse of the veins in his temples, the shouting, panting, huffing, gasping, the moment when he took his famous English whip down from the wall and started to beat me with it, the harsh rush of the leather lash, the thud, the light that sifted sideways through the bedroom window, the shadow of the oak tree dappling the rose bushes outside, the slipping outside of myself to a gray place above my body and soul and watching from the ceiling as he pushed me down on my back and peed on me, and then he locked me in the wardrobe. I remember every detail, every motion and sound and smell. I was in shock. I was going cold, dying. In the morning he opened the wardrobe and I slumped onto the floor like a hank of yarn. There was no feeling in my hands or feet. They felt like they'd been cut off. I curled up in a little ball like a fetus in the womb with my blinded eyes shut tight. It was involuntary. My body did it, as if it thought that position could protect me from all the evil. I lay there like I'd died of fright and terror and he picked me up gently and laid me on the bed and said in a fake, easygoing voice, Time to go to sleep, my little sweetheart. And soon he was snoring next to me, and I was a ravaged torso. I was so ashamed of myself and the state I was in that I squeezed my fists so tight they bled. I was ashamed that the Colonel had cheated on me with another woman. I was ashamed because I understood the trap I was in. I was ashamed at how childish and naive I had been. I was ashamed at my stupidity, that I hadn't believed what I'd been told. I was shut up inside my body for days, like I'd been encased in concrete. I couldn't feel anything, couldn't eat or sleep. Both of my eyes were swollen shut. My lips were split and stuck together. The Colonel was alarmed and tried to make up with me, but I was way beyond making up. He made me drink a glass of milk that he'd mixed with some kind of sedative, and I sank into a long, deep sleep.

When I woke up a day later, he was sitting on the edge of the bed. He tilted his head and looked at me and said, Please forgive me, sweetheart. I'm hopeless. There's a poisonous snake wriggling inside me. I've got an ant's nest where my brain should be. I'm at my wits' end. All our ideals have been kicked to the ground, everything beautiful destroyed. Russia and America are divvying up the world and spitting on us and making us lick the Russians' asses, and the Finnish people are such pitiful, stupid, disgusting sacks of shit. They never really were good deep down. The whole human race is just a big cunt full of lice. If I believed in God I'd pray to him to destroy the planet. And then he cried hard for a long time. I cried too. He promised that he'd never hit me again and he carried me to the sauna, which he'd already warmed up for me. He took off my bloody clothes and laid me down on a bench. I started to feel something in my hands and feet again. He looked over every inch of my body with a magnifying glass and called me his lithe little poetess. He shared some advice with me. Just like his father had with his mother. He said, You should always think only of pretty things, things that ennoble a person and make a woman more desirable, attractive, and lovable. And always think of faithfulness because it will help you develop love inside and help you suffer and submit and humble yourself and forget yourself.

Over the next several beautiful days I gradually regained my affection for him. The Colonel was so loving to me, and his safe, familiar voice softened me. Faith and hope had to return, because without them I would've died. It wasn't long until we were awash in a sea of forgiveness, like the thousand and one other hard things I pushed down inside me, the evil deeds. They sank like a sinful, polluted sack of stones. I remembered what my uncle Matti said, that you should never fight evil with evil. Evil will destroy itself. But I never had another orgasm with him again.

After the first time he hit me, the pattern of our life was always the same. Everything would be normal and good for a few days, and then the Colonel would get restless, couldn't breathe. He would feel like he was suffocating, poisoned by discontent, by desires even he didn't understand. It was like he had malaria, the sheets wet with his sweat, tossing and turning, starting awake, flailing around, until eventually he would leave the house. Go and screw who knows who, and come home drunk. Wake me up, criticize me, shout and pester and start a fight. If he had to, he'd fight by himself, work himself up into a fury and pound the wall with his fist. He would tear me out of bed, erupting with hate. He needed those fits of rage to get rid of what vexed him. Subjugating the weak made him feel good, soothed him, filled him with a sort of hubris that made his dick stand up. Then he would go out and cheat on me. I didn't dare to defend myself. I thought, I'm sure he'll calm down eventually. I thought it would get better, but it got worse and worse. He hated my submissiveness, hated the exact qualities that he'd loved when we were engaged. I didn't realize that evil was winning the fight and good was in retreat, even though he told me so in plain words. I was covered in scrapes and bruises, so he hid me from other people. If somebody came to visit and asked about me he would lie and tell them I was out picking berries or mushrooms or out skiing, and I'd be locked in a back room.

I would wash the dishes, and he'd say the glasses were dirty. I wash them again, and he says, There's streaks on them. So I wash them again. Now they're not shiny enough. I polish every glass with a dishcloth for half an hour. They'll do. I make reindeer and mashed potatoes. The reindeer's too dry and bland. I give it to the dog and make some more. That goes to the dog too. We eat just the potatoes and he thanks me with a fart. I make the bed. He says the comforter's crooked. I smooth it out. Still not good enough, the pillows look lumpy under the comforter. I make the whole bed up again. He says, You don't even know how to make a bed. I do the laundry. He says I hung them to dry wrong. Even though I hung them up the way he told me to. He tears the laundry off the line and strews it on the ground. I mop the floor. He complains that it's wet. I get a dry mop and go over it again. He inspects it and says it's not good enough.

He made me swear to keep my mouth shut about what was happening. No one could know what went on inside our four walls. Respect my dignity, he said. I didn't understand what he meant by that. Now I think the Colonel's dignity was the same thing as his poor self-esteem. He was so broken he couldn't approach any person, or any animal, as an equal. That was his fatal flaw. Love is a divine secret, he said; it has to be hidden from outsiders, and if you break that rule I'll kill you with my own two hands. Remember that.

I was so submissive I didn't even dare to tell Rebekka about any of it. I kept my mouth shut. As if I were ashamed for him. He wouldn't have even needed to hit me. He'd had me in his grip ever since he first came to see me at the school in Hirttojärvi. He had controlled me since I was four years old.

When he went to work I could breathe easier for a while, but if he was away for more than a day I'd have horrible pangs and miss him. Then he'd come back and I'd be shaking, nervous and afraid. He would huff and sigh and bang things, blast the radio, pace around and cuss and act like he needed a fix, and then leave and slam the door behind him. When he came home later, whether he was drunk or not, he'd start talking all about how he'd cheated on me with this one or that one and what a sweet little cunt this one or that one had. Sometimes he'd force me at knifepoint to sit on his lap and make me wallow in all his awful experiences and all the wickedness he'd done in the world. He'd make me listen over and over to how he'd raped that seventeen-year-old girl in Karelia and strangled her with his own hands and how good it felt back then and how horrible it felt now, how tortured he was by the bloody sins he'd committed.

I know from my own self that when rage comes busting out of a person, it cleanses them. If you don't let a bad feeling out it can poison you—you can even die from it. The cursing would subside, along with the slamming doors and throwing dishes and smashing furniture. The rage nibbled and gnawed at him till his nerves were shredded. He was infuriated by his own weakness, the fact that he'd abandoned his own people and left them to the mercy of the Germans, and at the same time he was scared for himself, not knowing if he would be tried as a Nazi for war crimes or get a clean slate and live a normal life.

I comforted myself with the thought that everything would be better once we got over our memories of the war and accepted that it was over, and we lost. I told myself that the Colonel was disappointed in democracy and bitter at the military. That was the reason for the beatings, and over time they would stop. I thought he had to let his anger out or he might have a heart attack and die. I didn't want that to happen. I thought that I could get through it. That the Colonel's love would gradually be cleansed and deepened and become an even greater love than it was before. That the respect that forms the basis of everything between two people would come back. That even the hardest times in life feel like happiness if you have courage and you think alike and are heading in the same direction. I was so desperate I even thought that if I could just become a mother it would give me power and faith and help me keep my life going, that being a father would make the Colonel a better man, that if I was a mother my son would be a man of peace.

After he beat me we would always cry together like little kids. We'd cry about the horrible trap we were in, and then we'd pray for the agony to continue, sharp and alive. In his own sick way he loved me, so I didn't want to think about leaving him. If you have love, even a sick love, you have everything.

But I got older, and the blood sport got to be too much for me. I eventually hit a wall, though it took a long time. About twenty years.

The feeling of doom spread to everything. The house in Tammisaari was always cold and dark, even when the sun was shining in a clear blue sky. The darkness came from inside me. For a while I tried my best to build a community with the wives on the base like I had at the border station. I held sewing circles where we looked at pictures of Germans burning the towns of Lapland. We would eat scones and sweet rolls and draw lots with lengths of yarn, and the winner would get a tiger cake. The other women would have sewing bees, sauna nights, parties where the men would wear their uniforms with the top buttons open and get tipsy and dance with their wives to foxtrot records they'd bought in Germany. I would participate when my face wasn't bruised.

At first we went to the parties together and came home in good spirits. But then the Colonel started wanting me to leave early while he stayed to drink some more and smoke his pipe. That meant he was going to fuck some other woman.

Even Christmas at Tammisaari was black, the land crusted with a dim glow of frost. Drops of slush fell from the sky and froze in an hour or two, covering the dark ground in a sheet of ice. It filled me with a deep, heavy longing for Lapland. For Christmas we built a big bonfire in the yard out of old branches and enjoyed the peaceful Christmas feeling in the light of the fire. Even after the war was over, ordinary people had to do without all sorts of things, especially coffee and rubber bands, but we had everything a person could ever think of needing—Swiss chocolate, English marmalade, Swedish sugar. I never needed a ration permit or coupons when I went to buy new fabric or a pair of nylons.

The last fall we spent at Tammisaari, I was expecting a son. I was forty-three years old and had never gotten pregnant, but in the middle of our shared hell, I did. I was awfully conflicted about it. On the one hand I was happy about the baby that was coming, but on the other hand I was terrified, thinking, What if the Colonel starts hitting not just me but the child too? I mulled for weeks about how to tell him. Then one morning after I'd screwed him all the way to his eyeballs I told him, We're gonna have a kid. He looked at me like you would a piece of rotten meat and said, You can't get knocked up, you're a barren old woman. I told him I'd been to the doctor and there was no doubt about it. He said, Well, go get rid of it. Now. He wasn't going to bring some poopy-pants kid into this shitty world. I said, You can't be serious. You can't deny me this happiness. Yes I can, he said, and he told me he'd call a doctor he knew who could handle killing a fetus. I started crying and he called the quack. There was no mercy. I went to the doctor and told him I didn't want an abortion. And what about your husband? the doctor asked. You're a married woman. Your opinion doesn't matter.

I was told to come the following week. I went straight from the doctor to the telegraph office and secretly called Rebekka and told her everything and we cried together. Rebekka said I could come live at her place in Helsinki for the whole pregnancy and she would make sure everything went well and the fetus could grow and be born in peace. I went home with this secret idea. The Colonel was nice to me and tried every which way to make it up to me. He explained that he couldn't approve of having a child because he'd be a horrible father. I said, You'll be a better person once you have your own son. You'll fall in love with him as soon as you lay eyes on him. He looked at me and he said it wasn't about whether he would change or not; it was about the fact that fathers always kill their sons. I said, What about Tea and Rudolf? You've been good to them. You don't understand anything, he sighed. Children are a reflection of death. Then he gently took my hand in his and said, My little poetess, don't think too much. Just trust me like you always have.

He was right. He would have been even more horrible to his own kid than he was to Rudolf. He had, after all, been really cruel to that poor boy. After the trip to Germany during the war, Rudolf hadn't come to see us once, even though the Colonel invited him. But I did run into him once. It was in the late '50s, two years after Kekkonen was elected president. Rudolf came up to me on the street, shook my hand warmly, and we chatted. He said he was on a trip to do some fishing and university business. He'd just been made a docent at Helsinki University. He talked for a long time about how the Colonel's deep malice and bitterness grieved him. Tea, on the other hand, never seem bothered by the Colonel's bitterness. She came from Sweden, where she worked as a doctor, to visit at the Villa many times, flitting through the rooms like a butterfly. When Tea came, the Colonel would become a completely different person, the way he used to be when we were engaged. He would chatter with her, always in Swedish—as if I couldn't understand them—and laugh and hum German marches and sometimes dance a little. Tea would gaze at him like he was some great benefactor, batting her eyes at him. She had his eyes and lips. I would sit in the kitchen by myself and cry.

Two days before the abortion appointment, and one day before my planned escape to Helsinki, General Talvela had a St. Stephen's Day party. We walked there hand in hand, in love. We stayed late into the evening and I watched as the Colonel chased down the general's cousin's daughter, who was barely twenty, and rooted at her behind the curtains. Afterward he looked at me like he was some conquering ladies' man, defiantly battling his impotence. I thanked the general and slunk home by myself, hurt and offended. The Colonel caught up to me and grabbed hold of me when I got to our porch. He tore my coat off, threw me on the floor, and punched me in the face. The next two minutes felt longer to me than any I ever lived through. He choked me until I passed out. My last thought was, I'm going to die. He kicked me in the stomach. Then, when I was lying in a horrible puddle of blood, my clothes torn, unconscious, he called a cab that took me to the hospital. I woke up there the next morning and couldn't feel myself. I'd tried to make the Colonel happy, and I'd failed completely.

I lay in the hospital ward for three months, suffering from loss of blood, of course, and also pneumonia, and I fell so low that I couldn't get out of bed. Rebekka came to visit me and she said afterward that I didn't react to anything. I was frozen like a stone, breathing hard, my hands shaking like an old woman's. That's known to happen when you're reacting not just to a physical attack but also a psychological one. While I was in the hospital the Colonel stayed in Tammisaari and bought himself a big timbered house by the river near Rovaniemi, which he christened the Villa. Naturally he hired Hulta Häkki to be his housekeeper. When my body was more or less recovered the old doctor wanted to send me straight home to my husband. His advice was that I should try to protect my head from being kicked.

Alatalo came to pick me up, and I told him to drive me to the Oulu Psychiatric Hospital. He said, Are you serious? I said I was. He believed me, and drove me to Oulu. But they wouldn't admit me, even when I told them how our Christmas celebration had gone from a nativity scene to a crucifixion.

I cried all the way from Oulu to Rovaniemi. All around me were signs of the war, although a lot of places that were burned to the ground had already been cleared away and rebuilt. The Colonel came out to greet me affectionately. He took me in his arms and kissed away my tears. I eventually calmed down, and was gradually tamed again. That's what people do. You're drawn to what you're used to and terrified of anything new. I knew what to expect with the Colonel, but I didn't know what to expect without him.

After I came home from the hospital, the Colonel was once again the center of everything. The same couple of dozen people, the cream of humanity, buzzing around him just like before the war. They all acted like there'd never been any war or any Germans at all. That crowd gave me a pretty sour welcome. So did Hulta Häkki. She'd once been Katri's faithful servant, after all, and she thought of me as a little slut till the day she died. They called me crazy. And they called me a whore. The Colonel, on the other hand, was a hero in the eyes of some prominent people in town. Nazi sins were forcibly forgotten and we blended in with the swarms of Americans bustling around Lapland. President Kekkonen, who was the justice minister back then, decided that Marshal Mannerheim wouldn't be charged with anything, that he wasn't responsible. Poor Airo and the rest of the combat leaders got all the blame. The Reds put up a stink, of course. Why should Mannerheim get special treatment? But they were told it was because the man was so sick—in his head and his body—that they didn't dare show him in public for fear it would put the security of the nation at risk. Poor Edwin Linkomies, the prime minister during the Continuation War, finished up his jail term and was immediately forgiven for all the sins of the National Socialists, and made president of the university. The past was scrupulously downplayed. Even old Emperor Hillilä was brought back, clean scrubbed and brand new.

I figured since we hadn't killed ourselves we might as well start getting used to the new way of doing things. I wrote to Rebekka, and she felt the same way. I figured people are like rats; they can adapt to anything. I remember I was at an event at the Lyceo auditorium and I said that the Russians were good singers and dancers. Better than the Germans. The next year I even joined the Soviet Club, just like Prime Minister Paasikivi and Rebekka. The Colonel said, My little poetess wants to secure a place in the cultural life of Russki Finland. I said, Life goes on.

Little by little I got my head turned around to a new point of view. I started to think that Germany had been rescued from Nazism and that the war was all the Germans' fault, that it was their precious violence that had given us all these ruined cities. I felt no pity for them. Now I think that Nazism didn't end when Hitler killed himself. I think that, given a chance, new Nazis and fascists will spring up, because that's how people are. They keep repeating the same mistakes and expecting different results. There's loving-kindness inside all of us, but it sits side by side with cruelty, heartlessness, and indifference.

The years passed and I was more or less one of the living again. Everybody could see that I was really low, of course, but they didn't make anything of it. Sometimes the Colonel would whisper in my ear, We'll get through this together, just the two of us. We don't need any doctors or head shrinkers butting into our business. The Colonel wasn't working after he left Hanko. He was always home, which was really tough on me. He didn't have anybody to pick on or abuse except me, his jumpy, despised little woman. I had ringing in my ears and not a thought in my head, just empty holes.

In the years after the war Lapland was different, the whole place buzzing with Americans, even the lumber camps. Me and the Colonel were at the market square once buying some smoked meat when who should slide up beside us but General Wallenius. He flicked his eyes at the Colonel like he was about to say something, but then he turned away. The Colonel picked up his package of meat and Wallenius picked up his, and we went about our business feeling sort of embarrassed. They were a couple of boys who'd done some bad things, all sorts of foolishness that was better forgotten.

And then there were those moments of light, when we went up to the top of a ridge and looked down at the country below, cradling its deep rivers, or when we'd be out fishing in some river valley surrounded by milky, spring-flooded lakes and swamps and see the hilltops rising up, or when we went rambling over the Lapp fells where the fog was thick as pea soup for two weeks running. We both loved the wild forest and tundra, the landscape as beautiful as a desert, nothing but undulating hummocks and boulders and scree in every direction. Sometimes we'd spend a week sleeping in a tent or a lean-to looking up at the reindeer constellation that the Frenchman Le Monnier had found and named when he set up his telescope at the top of Aavasaksa, and we'd talk about how to build the best bear's den or how to nurse a sick swan without getting blood on its feathers. We would laugh together at people's simplemindedness, stupidity, ignorance, ugliness, and gullibility. And yes, we could also laugh sometimes at our own crooked, cockeyed, stupidly proud ways of thinking. We rowed across tranquil lakes, fished for perch through the ice, counted the points on the snowflakes, gathered dew in a cup on an August morning, traveled around our country and around the world. Without these flashes of pure love I would have killed myself. I didn't have a single friend I could talk with honestly about the cruel reality I was living. Rebekka tried to help me from Helsinki, but it was hard with the Colonel always close enough to listen.

❖ ❖ ❖

The last time the Colonel beat me was when I made him some coffee and sandwiches. I carried them in on a tray and put them in front of him like I always did. He said, Put some sugar in the cup. I said, There isn't any. He threw the tray with the cups on it against the wall, grabbed me by the hair, and dragged me across the floor. I recall that Hulta was watching this torture from the kitchen door with apparent relish. Her eyes shone with excitement. She must have thought, Now he's finally going to kill that cockroach, and she could become the lady of the house. She never did, though. She choked on a wheat roll a couple of months later and died. Hulta lived her whole life through without ever thinking about what it meant. The Colonel never got another housekeeper.

I lay there on the floor and the world went black and I lost consciousness. The Colonel was alarmed and called Alatalo to come and take my limp body to his doctor's house, like he'd done many times before. The doctor couldn't get me to wake up. So he had to send me to the hospital. There happened to be a doctor on duty who had the guts to see what was going on. He was from the South, filling in. He asked me if my husband had done this. I said, Yes, and it's not the first time. He asked how long it had been going on. I said, Since the fall of 1944. He took care of my broken bones, but when he couldn't get the mouse's squeak out of my ears he sent me to the Oulu Psychiatric Hospital. I spent the first two weeks there vacant, staring at the ceiling. The third week they started giving me the treatment prescribed by my doctor, Konrad von Bagh. He was a doctor with the Lahti observation unit, an expert in military psychology. I was given lots of different kinds of treatment: insulin shots, cold baths, cardiazol injections, and electric shock. That perked me up enough that I was able to try to hang myself, with a perfect length of bandage, in a hospital bathroom that stank of sweat, pee, and rancid lard. I got caught and they tied me to my bed. I didn't put up a fight. I saw and experienced things there that I'd rather not say any more about.

In the bed next to me was a woman named Hilkka Adenauer. She was a nurse from the Vietonen School with chalky teeth and a crooked nose. We started to chat. She reminisced about her mother, me about my father. How one year at Midsummer he said, Let's go to the top of Aavasaksa to see the nightless night. So we jumped on a bus and by the time we got there snow was coming down in a drizzle and the sun was just barely dangling at the edge of the sky. Back then there was nothing but a little path to the top leading through thick woods. We climbed hard, and I was getting worn out. Dad picked me up on his back. The other kids had to keep climbing, even though it was tough going. We crossed a big patch of scree on both sides of the trail, then more climbing through deep forest. When we finally reached the top, the view across the miles to Torniojoki stopped my breath. We skipped down onto the northeast slope, which was a steep, steep boulder face, and threw rocks over the edge, and it was fun. Dad saw an eagle's nest and said, Be good or the eagle will come and carry you off.

Hilkka kept squeaking from the next bed, Tell me more.

I told her the story about Dad's crazy idea that he and all us kids should put on Lapp clothes, take a few old Lapps and reindeer with us as an exhibit, and go stand out in front of the zoo in Berlin and Warsaw and St. Petersburg. We would set up a *kota* like a summer encampment and show the people how the Lapps live. He was thinking we could make some money at it. So we all got on a train in Rovaniemi. I went along too. I was three years old. We got to St. Petersburg, and the reindeer caught spotted fever and started dying one by one before we'd even set off from the train station. It took us two days of searching to find the zoo, and the men started setting up the *kota*. Then a local official came up and asked us for our permit. Dad had his papers in order, but the men were all taken to jail anyway. Us kids and the women were left there cry-ing our eyes out as people stood around watching. Some of them threw us a ruble or two. We might've died one by one ourselves if a Finn hadn't showed up and arranged with the prosecutor to get us a ride back to Rovaniemi. Dad and the Lapp men came home a few weeks later all hungry skin and bones. One had come down with typhus he got from who knows where, and another one'd caught something from the water and they didn't have anything to treat it but homemade rotgut, tar-water, and hot reindeer blood.

In the mental hospital the world seemed like such a strange place. The void of death was loudly calling to me, but I wasn't ready. I started to feel like lying there was good for me. I didn't have to do anything, just surrender to those Mengeles' manipulations and keep my mouth shut. But eventually the day always comes when you get driven out of paradise and commanded to recover.

One morning Bagh came and stood by my bed. He ran his tongue over his teeth, gave me an impish look, and said, You know what you are? You're full of yourself. You're a melodramatic, phony bitch, a morally corrupt, feeble excuse for a human being, and if the Nazis had won the war I'll bet you'd be minister of culture right now. But sadly, that's not to be your fate. You don't get to lie around living off the government. From now on you're going to have to take charge of your own life, and if you kick up any fuss about it I'll give you a whipping and send you to hard labor till you start begging me to send you back to the Colonel.

I fell apart. I was so deeply shocked by what he said that it forced me to start my long, difficult resurrection.

First I learned to breathe, to live through each bright day, hot or dry or dark or wet. I ate well and gathered the strength that in my dejection I had lost completely. Then, when I'd rebuilt my breath and learned to eat all the food on my plate and not just nibble at it, Rebekka came all the way from Helsinki to see me and she said, Let's put this cat on the table and go over it hair by hair, because you've got to get yourself free of the Colonel, body and soul. I said, You're right, but how? Life has glued the two of us together. I couldn't get away from him if I stood on my head. Then Rebekka said she was going to tell me some things that would help me get back in the water, like a fish—or back in the air, if I was a fly, whichever. She told me about all the things the Colonel did to her back in Rovaniemi, in our own house, and the shame she'd carried with her, and how she'd got herself out from under it. When I heard about all that, it brought up a kind of poison in me, and I was finally able to leave the hospital. I was full of anger. I planned a swift revenge. Sometimes it was a calm, decisive settling of scores—I would go to the Villa like nothing was unusual, and I would shoot the Colonel while he sat in his easy chair, or shoot him in both hands and take my Sami knife and cut off his dick and stuff it in his mouth and let him suffocate. I made all kinds of plans, day and night, and it made me stronger. I realized later, of course, that malice and revenge would hurt me more than it did him. He wanted to die. His whole life was foreplay with Old Mister Cold.

Getting free from the Colonel seemed like an impossible, faraway dream at first. The whole idea scared me to death. I thought if I left the Colonel I'd die of grief. Then I just started saying to myself, I can think about the Colonel tomorrow. And that's what I did. I just put off thinking about him for one more day, and then another. And it worked. I would do it for a minute, an hour, a day at a time, and slowly but surely I started to believe that I really could live alone—and if I couldn't, I'd get myself a few dogs and cats. What I grieved the most was that giving up the Colonel meant giving up my rank. I wouldn't be a colonel's wife anymore. When I cried about this to Rebekka, she said there's no law says you can't use his name and call yourself a colonel's wife till the day you die.

It took me three years to unload the rocks off the sled I'd been pulling behind me all my life. Every time I'd toss a chunk off I'd feel a little stronger. Because deep down, I'm really a healthy, normal person. Still, it took me by surprise when Bagh came to my room one day and shoved a piece of paper in my hand that said: *biliosis, melancholicus, cholerius, complexio cholerica*. And at the bottom: *ingenium bonum*. I was put out of the hospital and went to Helsinki to live with Rebekka and try to get used to normal life. Rebekka taught me all over again how to cook porridge, how make a macaroni casserole, how to hold a pen in my hand.

From Helsinki I got a job as a teacher at a school in a place called Raatasuo—Carcass Swamp. They gave me the job because I was the only applicant.

With Tuomas, who was just a kid himself, I could start over from scratch and rebuild myself. We grew up together.

I could build a new sexuality.

THE CARCASS SWAMP SCHOOL was way out in the woods, in a little village perched on the side of a ridge. I was told that if you had a boat and were a good rower you could get there in a couple of hours, but on foot from the main road it was more than ten kilometers, way out in the deep woods. A war-starved combat veteran and avowed Red and his flock of hungry kids, the poorest of the poor, would be there to meet me.

I wasn't scared. I've loved bogs and wild forests ever since I was little, and the name of the place warmed my heart. The metropolis of Ylitornio and the border with Sweden were close by, too, which of course made the place much more interesting. The people in the area had a colorful history. And there were all the great rivers and lakes near there, and a string of high blue hills around it.

A week before school was supposed to start I got off a bus on the side of the road and set out through the woods. I had just one bag with a few ragged clothes inside. Tagging along behind me was my friend Eva Braun, a genuine Persian cat. I'd got her from Ragnar Lassinantti, the resident governor of Norbotten Province, at a party a few days earlier. We'd had a wonderful evening at a hotel in Haaparanta, and when I woke up in the morning there was a cat in my room. She had a red ribbon around her neck with a tag that said, *With love from your eternal friend Ragnar.* I sniffed at her and stared at her for a long time, trying to think who she reminded me of. That's where her name came from. And now we were trudging down a road that skirted along the edge of the hill country until it came to a bare place, then turned toward the little village. The whole way there I felt like I was one with the landscape.

I arrived to find a just-built, cobbled-together settlement that smelled like fresh-sawed lumber, and all around it a wild, unbroken marsh that stretched for thousands of hectares, filled with water-birds and fish spawning grounds, part bog, part open water, smelly and overgrown—basically an impossibly perfect, beautiful Finnish swamp sea. There were reeds, heather, cotton grass—and cloud-berries, of course. I thought, This is the kind of out-of-the-way spot that's a sanctuary for plants and animals. And for me. I fell in love with the place, the ancient gleaming dusk where light fades fast to shadow.

I sat in the dark little teacher's apartment with Eva Braun, listen-ing to Wagner, the music as fresh and deep as the August evening.

Tuomas told me later that the people in the village had been horrified all summer that their new teacher was going to be a woman who used to pal around with some SS bigshot. A high-class whore. A colonel's mattress—for a colonel everybody knew was a wife beater, a drunken, whip-wielding gun toter, and, even worse, a Finland-Swede, born and raised in Helsinki. Somebody said they'd heard that this Nazi slut also fancied herself a writer. Tuomas was intrigued by these reports. He'd been in a fever all summer to see the woman of ill repute they'd got for themselves. He said he'd snuck up to the school several times in the days be-fore I arrived to peek in the windows and see if anyone was mov-ing around in there.

When he finally did see me in the schoolroom, his legs gave out and he peed his pants. I beckoned to him and he ran in so fast he tripped on his way through the door. He asked me where the Colonel was. I whispered in his innocent ear that the Colonel was so long gone I could hardly remember him.

Tuomas was just fourteen years old, but he was full grown, tall and handsome, very blond but with eyes almost as black as mine. Hungry eyes. We went for a walk in the woods, me in front and him following behind, and we both had the same thing in mind.

We walked until we found the widest, prettiest part of the marsh. We stood on a bobbing raft of weeds and took off all our clothes. Tuomas took off everything but his drawers. We lay down on our backs, side by side, and I watched the clouds drift by. Tuomas's eyes were closed. I put my hand on his chest, very lightly, and he opened his eyes. There was a gleam in them that was easygoing, but electric. I moved my hand lower and slipped three fingers under the elastic band of his underwear. His dick sprung straight up. I looked at his face. He grinned at me, and I thought, There he is. There was a ray of light in his eyes that I could feel right down to my toes. At first I was thinking, It's wrong to get involved with a kid, but then I thought, He sure looks like a man to me. I got on top of him and the moment his dick slipped inside me, I came. It made me laugh, but I acted like it was nothing and we kept going.

I didn't have to teach Tuomas anything. He did everything instinctively. He was glowing from within like the northern lights, murmuring some song in my ear while he thrust into me. He was like an elk when it feels in its blood that rutting time has come, when it smells the call of it coming over the land. Like he had always mated, even though it was probably his first time. His fluids flowed into me and he fucked me over and over, with the water in the marsh splashing. He was like a goat fucking every pussy in the whole world. I came again and again and I felt like I would empty out and die. But I didn't die. That first time we had sex there was such a pure, innocent passion of love, an explosive charge that came from somewhere back in the Stone Age, and when we lay back down, weak and meek and happy under the crazy beautiful shimmering blue sky I said, Let's give Carcass Swamp a new name. Let's call it Happiness Swamp.

Later, in the middle of the night, I was alone in the teacher's apartment and I looked out the window. The moon shone through the branches of the old spruce trees, the shadows stretching toward the coming winter. I thought, We've written a promise of love on the waters of the swamp, into the memory of the earth, and now my third life can begin. I'm going to experience another time of innocent, tender affection, like I had in the early days with the Colonel, and maybe this will be a love where I won't have to keep my mouth shut. I loved the desire and the pleasure and the feeling of belonging together and needing each other. The real love.

The thing with Tuomas was, his young cock just went right to my head. I'd been force-fed on an old man's shriveled, half-hard dick that smelled disgusting. Tuomas's young, healthy sperm smelled good. His whole self had such a young, fresh smell. I was buoyant. All the weight of life evaporated. There was just an indescribable feeling of floating in the arms of the night. We were like two crazy kids, just like it'd been with the Colonel long ago, before the pastor said the Amen and blessed our marriage. I did all the things to Tuomas that the Colonel had done to me when we were secretly engaged for all those years, and Tuomas was putty in my hands.

I did notice that the more people talked about the Colonel, the more satisfied Tuomas became. It stoked his ego to know he was fishing the Colonel's patch. He had young blood and all his powers. He was a bear and the Colonel was a dried-up rotten old mushroom. A real Nazi might've said that the Colonel was a good man who wasn't afraid of anything, that even on the front he'd pressed on with no regard to cold or hunger or exhaustion. But that opinion of him was pretty rare. Even the old White Guards bawled about how he'd purposely let the Red partisans through at Seitäjärvi at the end of the war, said he was a bald-faced traitor to both the Nazis and the Russians. They told stories about how he'd acted like the devil himself toward the civilian guards, flogging and torturing them in training, how he'd killed some beautiful young boys, and especially girls, for no reason at all during the war. There were rumors that he'd set the Sami fighting against their own people at Petsamo, the Inaris against the Kolts. That may have been true, but whenever anyone bad-mouthed the Colonel I defended him. I felt like I was the only one who had the right to murder him.

Tuomas started living with me at the school. I wondered if we ought to keep it secret, but then I decided that everybody has a right to live their life. During the day he would go from my apartment to the classroom, where he was my pupil. He got average grades, but was good at drawing.

There were two of us teaching at the school. The villagers were all Reds, but both of us teachers had been on the side of the Whites. I taught the lower grades and Jaakko, a traveling Laestadian preacher and heavy drinker from Tornio, taught the older kids. He was a handsome man, like preachers tend to be. He had a large, serious nose, and a head of black curly hair. The people in the village said he had Sami and Swedish blood flavored with a bit of Russki or French. Jaakko was a binge drinker. When he was drinking he'd keep a bottle in the teacher's desk and take swigs from it all day long. It didn't harm his teaching any, and the kids liked him better when he was soused. When he was sober he had a quick temper.

The students were humble, shy, well-behaved kids used to hard work. They were also wild, reckless, undisciplined little barbarians. The war had made them that way. Their fathers and brothers had been sent to the front and they'd gotten used to a permanent state of emergency, never knowing who was going to die in combat, who would catch a disease, who would be a hero. For them, the war had been an adventure as much as it was a constant fear of who'd be next, and you could see it in them.

My classroom was cold and damp, like all classrooms up north. Just outside the walls was a dense forest of spruce trees reaching for the sky. I watched the seasons change twice a year. When I held class inside, the students would sit sullen at their scratched-up two-person desks. I was at a tall desk in the front, with a blackboard behind me. My desk had a black writing slate, a blotter with black and blue stains on it, and a bottle of paste. Three lightbulbs hung from the ceiling and buzzed, casting just enough light into the corners to let the kids read their primers. On the back wall Jaakko had hung some beautiful elk horns and above them a Suomi submachine gun with the clip removed. And then there was the smell. The kids always smelled like wet felt—like filth, to be honest. Back then people took a sauna once a week at most, and in the cold of winter once a month if you were lucky. I would splash the Chanel No. 5 that the Colonel had given me on my neck and hands every morning to make it through the day. The kids used to sniff at it in ecstasy. To them it was an enticing, exotic smell. I was so glad to have my own money. I could use my pay however I liked. I was used to having to beg every cent I needed from the Colonel, even for food.

Tuomas was an ordinary kid from a poor, communist village—tough, a bit on the quiet side. Now he's a chubby, lazy thing with a potbelly. He has a long beard and a bushy mustache like some maharaja, and Jesus hair hanging to his shoulders. But his balls don't hang down like the Colonel's did. If the Colonel saw Tuomas he'd be so jealous. The Colonel hated aging. He would have liked to be a supple, well-fed buck all his life.

Tuomas has become just like me inside and out. He is melded to me at the cellular level, body and soul. As a young husband he liked to lie around drinking beer and smoking cigarettes. Now when he comes over he always goes to the rocking chair and rocks. Before and after our divorce, in spite of the age difference, we've always been on the same page, except of course I come from better stock. No one's ever even worked out his family tree.

We were left in peace to live together in a pinky lock for two years. Living in the teacher's quarters, there in the heart of the open marsh, among the low red permafrost mounds and bright green leaves and hidden hollows, I gradually grew into myself. The whisper of the tall pines soothed and energized me; the squeak of the winter frost and the bubbling spring brooks made me believe I still had the strength to live. I came of age, became a female of rank who had seen many things. Like an elk. I became both male and female, became a thing I didn't even know I had in me. I had always thought I was more of a rough tuft of moss floating in a vinegar swamp, or maybe a sort of cow by nature, but I was actually growing a handsome crown of antlers, till everybody who crossed my path took one look at me and thought, Here's a woman who has a heart that a person should stop and get to know.

Tuomas was seventeen, working without pay as the school custodian, and I was almost fifty, a teacher and soon-to-be author when I proposed. I said, Why wait any longer? Let's make this thing official and give the president some paperwork. We had to get official permission because he was underage.

The people in the village had looked askance at us from the beginning. The whole atmosphere was like swimming in poison. When people heard from the school cook that I intended to marry Tuomas, they really threw a fit. It wasn't just the age difference or because Tuomas was a kid when I first let him into my bed. The way they saw it, my biggest sin was that I'd already been joined in the bonds of holy matrimony twice and gotten divorced—against the commandments of God—and now I had the gall to get married a third time, and to a mere child. Was there no limit to my shame? While I waited for the president to send us permission to marry, I wrote a book for kids. It won a whole slew of awards. News of it must have reached the president, because pretty soon our permission slip arrived in the mail.

We got married at the Kemi magistrate's, without any ceremony. Right after that, Tuomas got a letter ordering him to appear for military service, of course. Tuomas said he had no intention of picking up a gun and he didn't want to be away from me for such a long time. He said, Can't you get me crazy papers? I mulled it over a little bit and sat up when I realized he didn't need crazy papers. I made a trip to HQ in Rovaniemi and after that Tuomas didn't get any more letters from the army. But the gossip just got thicker. If gossip could kill you I'd've died and rotted away a long time ago. I got fed up with backwoods village bad-mouthing, gave up teaching—and the regular paycheck—and devoted myself full-time to writing. I got a loan for this house, and we moved in together.

I figured out right away that a person can't live on what a writer makes. A penny here, a penny there, debts, bills. It was an awful letdown for me. I'm sure Tuomas didn't notice any difference, since he grew up in poverty, but I was used to nothing but the best, the life of a colonel's wife, and I was rattled. I made sure I didn't show it, though. I never let the facade slip. I have a bit of actress in me. I know my entrances and exits.

I had to get money, so I started doing all sorts of little speaking engagements. And to my surprise I turned out to be quite a good speech maker, a talent that earned me a pile of dough for groceries so we wouldn't go hungry. I let the loans slide. Banks have money to spare. I expanded my repertoire, started giving nature talks. In my heart I've always been more a part of nature than of humanity. I managed to stop them from putting a dam in on the Ounasjoki and fought the high rollers in the South who wanted to develop Lapland and exploit it till the end of time.

I've been asked a thousand and one times why I became a writer. It was in the stars. Back when I was little I had a horrible growth in my belly that had to be cut out. The operation went off without a hitch, but I didn't wake up from the anesthesia. I was out for a good week, and everybody thought I would die. Most of all

my mother, of course. Then I got hold of some little scrap of consciousness and I drifted to someplace on the gray line between life
and death. I remember seeing the eternal light of the kingdom of
heaven and beautiful angels beckoning to me and I was just about
to take hold of an angel's hand, but then I felt a sort of powerful
gust of wind that blew against my face and my hair and I pulled my
hand back. And I woke up and opened my eyes. I don't remember
it myself, but my godmother, a childhood friend of my mother's
who'd once been the governor's girlfriend, told me that the first
thing I said was, I'm going to be an artist. Everybody who'd been
there to see it started saying, That girl rose from the dead. My godmother examined my head and found a lump on the back of my
skull. She's got the painter's burl, she said.

When Rebekka was ten she found our mother's old music books
and taught herself to play the piano, Liszt and Bach, Beethoven,
Vivaldi. I tried, too, when I was thirteen, but I only managed to learn
part of the first song in the book, about flying up to the clouds. By
the time she was twelve Rebekka was reading Lagerlöf, Paulaharju,
Dostoevsky, Sillanpää, Lermontov, Tolstoy, Jotuni, Kant, Plato,
Strindberg. They were all on my dad's bookshelf. When I was fourteen I decided to wade through the classics. I started with Sillanpää,
got to page five, and quit. Too much hopelessness and rhyming for
my taste. I picked up Dostoevsky. Just an old man harping on religion. Strindberg seemed nuts to me, and I couldn't understand
a word of Kant. Selma Lagerlöf's *The Wonderful Adventures of Nils*
saved me. I read it cover to cover, over and over.

After we moved into our little blue cabin here I started writing
like crazy. The black mouth of the typewriter hissed and barked
and I watched its little sharp teeth bite the words onto the white
paper and a floaty feeling bubbled up inside me and I was just
bursting with certainty, like a plumped-up stamen in a flower. I
just sort of slid into the feelings and sensations of the characters

that came to life in the sentences I wrote. Time would fly by, and it would be night again. I don't remember ever eating or drinking on the days I was writing. Then when I would get up from the desk I would feel the world rushing toward me, trying to knock me over. I used to keep a glass of milk beside me on the desk to guzzle down in emergencies. It was creative nirvana, and so was the innocent love Tuomas had given back to me, the belief in life, the feeling of safety that had been lost since the day my dad died. Tuomas said, Just write like a White Guard butcher and it'll be good. So I started taking big ladles of stuff from my own life, like the great poets do.

I decided to write about me and the Colonel, and whenever I sat down at the typewriter it was just like when I used to hide from him and write in secret, even though I knew he was in Helsinki, probably dying, or already dead. But it felt like he was alive, like he was inside the typewriter and any minute he might jump out and grab me. I tried to keep my wits about me by talking out loud, saying, Listen here, you devil, when you and me were hitched I had nothing of my own, nothing but covering up for your sins and protecting you. But that's all over now. I was full of anger and vengeance, in the grip of some natural urge, like a wild deer. I felt like I was somebody else, like while I was writing I left myself behind and started taking my revenge, slicing off heads with a sharp sword. I got very close to the core of everything, dipped my ladle in the spring of truth. Although I did censor out the worst parts. The parts so obviously true that no one would believe them.

If I'd never written about my marriage to the Colonel, it would have been a sin and a crime. Keeping silent makes it so you can't get any food down your throat, or can't keep it down, so it just comes right out again at both ends. Keeping silent kills you from the inside out. Throughout the history of the world there have been those who tell and those who don't, because shame keeps them from speaking. Just think of Eva Braun. She never opened her mouth publicly, just went right on smiling behind her glass screen. Or the Führer's niece, the one who was a victim of sadism. She opened her mouth, and ended up killing herself.

Without the courage Tuomas gave me I would've kept quiet and gotten even worse; the holes in my body and soul would've started to sting and rot. But I put all the badness down on paper. I vomited it up, and it felt like all my teeth went flying out with it. I thought my marriage to the Colonel was, and would ever be, the center point of my life, that it would stamp my whole existence, on this earth and in heaven. Whenever a memory of the Colonel came into my mind I would clench up and sort of freeze right where I was, and my feet would tingle and go numb. It's all so deep inside me. Even now, when I think of him I feel a jab in my head like a stake going right through it, and my heart skips a beat.

I'm guessing that if it's well watered down, mine and the Colonel's story of suffering will sell, and I can make some money, which I'm always short on. So my typewriter keeps clattering. It'll be done soon.

My publisher pampers me. I have a drawer stuffed with cash. We've been to the Canary Islands and to Sochi to admire the sunshine. We took a taxi to Helsinki and stayed at Hotel Torni for a few days and drank. I'm constantly getting awards and accolades and clinking the blood-red crystal glasses from Russia that the Colonel's brother Johan gave me like it was nothing. I must've learned something from Maila Talvio's soirees after all. My face is on the cover of all the magazines, I'm interviewed on radio and TV about my own affairs and everybody else's, get invitations all the time to big cultural to-dos, even parties at the governor's house. I've covered myself in glory, and I'm content. I've never made any claims about the literary value of the stuff I write. I used to try to do as Maila would and throw parties here in my little blue cottage, but they were pretty thin affairs. People up north don't know how to have fun at a party. They just gobble down the food, slurp up the drinks as fast as they can, and leave.

I knocked a few of my books out in a hurry, and they weren't very good. I always thought the story was more important than the words. It seemed like the right idea at the time. Readers like a book you don't have to think about, just bang right through from start to finish. They don't want you to be profound or stir things up. I wrote books that would sell, and I have a drawer full of cash to show for it, but I couldn't do it anymore, couldn't think of any more good stories, and since I'm no stylist and not much good when it comes to the artistic side of writing, my sales started to fall. So I tried writing poems. But I gave that up. They didn't have any feeling or ideas to them. A lot of my writing is just fluff. I didn't want to waste people's time writing stuff that made them think. That's just adding to their troubles. Except for the nature books. Those have some subtlety to them. But the novels are the ones that put food on the table.

Sometimes Tuomas and I were hard up because of drink, and the lacy curtain of desolation would wrap itself around us. We never fought, even when we were on a real tear. Tuomas wasn't an arguer. He liked fishing, just like the Colonel. We fished, went picking berries and mushrooms. And when we were in Helsinki on writing business Tuomas would either walk quietly behind me, or right beside me in a pinky lock.

I'd like to remember my own beginnings,

search out my first joys and sorrows. My first childhood crush.

The old games. Being a teacher. Geraniums, train engines. A bridge, a tiny caterpillar.

THERE WAS SLEET THIS MORNING. I climbed out of bed and dragged myself over to the wardrobe mirror. A monster was staring back at me with crooked, bespectacled eyes, a flabby belly, a broken-down body. I thought, Is that me? What happened to the beautiful, attractive me I used to be? I studied myself awhile and pretty soon I felt better. I'm not ashamed of myself. I carry this old dying woman's body around with pride. Decay is the law of life, the circle of life decreed for all human creatures. The Colonel hated getting old. He was afraid he'd wake up one day and his desire would be gone and he wouldn't be able to get it up anymore.

I pushed the Colonel out of my head and made some coffee. I drank it slow, used up at least and hour, maybe two. I looked out the window at a reindeer cow I knew, wandering at the edge of the woods. I raised my hand and she nodded her head at me. In the olden days people thought animals were above us, because they understood things that humans know nothing about. That comforts me. And I'm the kind of person who's spread so wide in all directions that I end up liking my own company best. I'm my own vast marshland and sandy shore, my own swamp, damp and lush and unexplored. Sometimes I'm as inviting as warm sun at the edge of the garden, as sweet as a ripe ear of barley. I'm so intrigued by all the things living inside me that I can't muster any interest in anyone else. All the other people and their little lives seem so narrow compared to the life inside me, and it just grows more abundant as time goes by. Instead of other people I have my characters making their entrances and exits. And my dogs and cats, of course. They're easy to understand. People are considerably harder. My animals never talk about themselves, but they always listen to my chatter with interest. I've got my writing window over there, where the universe can look in on me, and I can stare out at the yard. In the summer it's a jungle, in the winter an unbroken blanket of snow. The window has sunk over the years till now it's nearly level with the ground, and fireweed has grown up against it, as lush and beautiful as I am. At midsummer the flowers sway in time with the gentle weather, bright colors all across the yard, deep violet, snow white, yellow, aniline red. I have the north light for company, and the floorboards that creak when the kitties and puppies pad across them. I go out in the yard and look at the sky, as far as I can see, and flocks of birds and clouds and wind are there with me. I always keep all the doors open. You can come in if you like.

Yesterday a reindeer buck came trotting out from behind the storage shed and then Tuomas appeared in the shed doorway. He said hello to all the critters first, taking his time, then walked over to the house. He looked me in the eye and said, You're hard at it. Tuomas is lazy compared to me, but that doesn't bother me. I had quite enough bustle and hurry in the old days with the Colonel. With Tuomas I've always enjoyed just being.

Before me and Tuomas got married I told him, Think about it first. My cooch is old and worn out. I can't give you any children. He said he didn't figure on any kids. Twenty years later he said he wanted to leave something behind in this world, at least one offspring. I said, I knew this was coming. It's OK with me, I told him, even though it broke my heart. I was laid low for a minute, but I got up again. I thought, If I leave it to Tuomas to handle this offspring thing, nothing's going to happen. I looked around and found an ad in the personals that sounded acceptable. I met her at the Kemi bus station before I brought her to meet Tuomas. She had black hair and black eyes like me, the same build as I had when I was young, and to top it off we were born on the same day of the same month. I asked her how old she was and she said she was eighteen and inexperienced. Her father was twenty-eight years older than her mother. Just like me and the Colonel. I'm twenty-eight years older than Tuomas. And he was eighteen when we got married. Everything repeats. Just the roles change. We had such a nice talk that she came home with me. Tuomas kicked at first and said she was just a kid and he would have to teach her everything. I said the younger she was the better the chances, and he stopped complaining. I made a deal with them that I would be godmother to all their kids. So me and Tuomas divorced and she and Tuomas got married and they had a baby within a year. Their flock of kids hasn't changed the bond between me and Tuomas at all. He comes over every day. He's attached to me, still in my flesh. He would be if we lived on different planets.

Before he officially left my house for the last time, we took a walk hand in hand out to our spot on Happiness Swamp. It was the middle of September in 1980, just before sunset, and we stood in that familiar place where the land and water meet and looked at the western sky. The sun dyed half the sky sulfur yellow and the whole swamp was reddish orange like it used to look on an icy night in the South. Blackbirds sang in the rotted branches, grebes and mergansers dove beneath the moss, and a pair of cranes slogged through the marsh grasses. We didn't say anything, just took off our clothes and laid them on our familiar boulder, waded in and meandered like a marsh caravan from hummock to hummock till we came to the eye of the swamp and lowered ourselves into the water that we'd come to love over the years. There in the embrace of the warm mud and slime and scum we watched the mist start to rise from the water and cover the land in thick, even layers. It covered over everything. We were in the middle of infinity. Just us. Nothing more. Melancholy, sad, joyful. A new beginning. We walked back in the arms of a night tinged with frost and Tuomas continued home to his bride. Our divorce was official a year later, but even though he lives there and I live here, we've always stuck together. The kids Tuomas fathered are always running around in the yard, or here in the house. I can't put up with their screaming for long, and Tuomas comes to get them. Then the house gets quiet again and the noise of the kids is nothing but a fresh smell left behind and my own childhood memories ambush me, in the form of objects. I remember my grandmother's big ladle lying on the dish counter, the yellow roses on the butter dish, the white pillowcase with gypsy lace, my mother's morocco shopping bag made from a camel's hide with a tooled picture of a caravan crossing the desert.

My first memory is of my mother's vegetable garden. The maid Olga was the one who really took care of it. I was probably about two, and Olga went out to the garden on a summer day to weed the carrots. I slipped out from under Rebekka's watchful eyes and toddled over to the edge of the garden to watch Olga, and the world. The garden was crowded with all kinds of plants leaning over on top of each other and twisted around each other, strangling the life out of each other, vining up the sauna wall to the roof, climbing the fence to spread across the dirt road and over to the cookhouse door. I went to lie down under a currant bush and dig in the dirt. I found chestnut beetles and dung beetles and black beetles and put them in my dress pocket. Then I fell asleep to the lullaby of buzzing flies. Rebekka says she and Olga looked for me for an hour. They ran down to the lakeshore and even to the river. Nothing. They were panicked, naturally, but they didn't dare tell my mother I'd disappeared. Finally Olga found me under the bush and carried me back to the house without making a sound.

My second memory is connected to a feeling between my legs like something breaking me in two. In that memory there's a man who sees a girl not yet a woman and has an urge to do that to her. A man who wields his cock and forces himself on an instinctively compliant little girl and entraps or even destroys her entire sexuality. All this dawned on me gradually later on, there in the loony bin at the end of the 1950s when I started talking with Hilkka, my fellow lunatic. First I realized that if I didn't talk about something, then it didn't exist. It wasn't until I dressed something in words that it became true. And then a memory came up of me secretly running to the house at the border station, in spite of my dad telling me not to, hurrying through the house without being seen, going to a room in the back of the house, and seeing the Colonel sitting at his desk and a neighbor girl named Inkeri standing on the desk with her checked apron held up to her ears and the Colonel putting three fingers into her underwear. I saw all this and turned and ran away.

Hilkka listened to me, was quiet for a minute, and then said, Did you ever think that maybe Inkeri was actually you?

I said, Don't be stupid.

But it left me thinking.

The neighbors didn't even have a kid named Inkeri.

The only thing I worry about now is whether I'll have enough firewood to last through the winter.

HERE IN MY LITTLE BLUE COTTAGE I'm as cozy a bug in a pike's belly. My soul has found peace. I like to just sit and cry for no reason. It cleanses me.

When me and Tuomas moved here the house was already half sunk in the wet ground and the corners were all askew. Down at the end of the yard is my pantry—a lake full of fish, left by the last ice age, long, shallow, and clear. I get tears in my eyes whenever I stand and look out at the woods and boulderlands on the distant shores around the lake and the hills rising to the sky like temple domes. I think about striving past generations in these wild places. They lived in a biblical paradise. They had food, and fire to keep them warm. On starlit nights they watched the same heavenly show that I watch now, listened to the same silent garden of stars, saw the same eerie, waxen, deathly pale sliver of moon at the heart of winter. Sometimes I smell ripening heads of grain, sometimes the fragrance of timothy hay, sometimes sprawling potatoes in bloom. Behind the house the forest begins, with its mysterious Black Ditch where the stones are copper colored and the water flows like gold. There's a healing spring there, too, and a crane nesting ground and a crumble-edged canal. These open spaces have seen millions of sunrises and they may see millions more if humans leave the earth in peace.

I've lived such a calm, tired life these past few years that it feels as if I don't even exist anymore. I think the inward journey will only grow. The feeling of disappearing is both terrible and wonderful. Add to it the anguish and pain of how humans treat the land and air and water, in other words, the nature of Lapland, which birthed all my books, and I feel a squeezing in my chest and my heart burns, like I'm drowning in the world's shit. When I get one of those spells of hopelessness I have a drink, or two, or a whole bottle and open another. I medicate myself with alcohol. It never fails me. It keeps me sturdy and safe. But I won't become a drunk, not as long as I keep writing. A book will yell to me from the typewriter, Put a cork in it and get to work! and I obey.

Every morning I wait for Tuomas. When I hear his footsteps on the porch my soul warms and my heart just hums with contentment. He starts the fire, carries in more wood and makes me some porridge, and we talk.

I forgive the Colonel for his individualism, his violence and arrogance, his blasphemy, ambition, duplicitousness and dishonesty, his disdain for moral duty, his shameless wealth, his generosity and stinginess. For being a wonderful Renaissance man, and a dirty lech. If I had to I could even forgive all the humiliations and kicks and whippings—easily— forgive the spiritual torture that drove me to the mental hospital. But I can never forgive him for beating our son out of me till he lay in a puddle on the floor of the porch. I will not, cannot forgive that.

I DON'T WANT TO REMEMBER THE COLONEL or think about him anymore. I'm so sick of the whole subject. I just want to focus on myself. The Colonel didn't trust anyone. He used to say that the worst thing in his life was other people. He didn't love anyone. He was just driven by his prick, and it never gave him a moment's peace. He had a Renaissance spirit in the sense that he loved literature and art and people being intelligent and well read. Sometimes he ate porridge for weeks at a time, with tinned meat mixed in, or nothing but raw potatoes with salt sprinkled on top. He liked to rush from one extreme to the other. In that way he had a Russian soul, even if he did hate Russians. He hated the Russian inside himself, just like the Führer hated the Jew inside him. Wallenius once told me that the Colonel was a coward, that in a pinch he would turn tail, and that was why he screamed and hit anyone weaker or lower than him every time he got the chance. And then he'd give presents to the same people he'd just humiliated. And me, poor kid, I admired, worshipped the man, although as he grew older his vitality started to fade, the current slowing down till he couldn't spray like a fountain of joy anymore. I could use all my slutty wiles on him and his limp cock would just hang there. He had no desire deep down. Lived alone like an animal.

He was driven by instinct to drool over a female and hunt her down until he got her in his trap, and then he'd start torturing and ridiculing her. It consoles me that this cold blue winter sky forgives everything, that this sky will last at least until the end of April. The cold will keep every living thing frozen and the snows will wipe away the boats and barns, the woodpiles and the flagpoles, like the Great Spirit has decreed. Then early spring will bring a southern wind and the ice will break up and it will pile up on the shores and a new life will start to emerge. That's how eternity created the world, opposites put together to make a whole, fit together like bratwurst with sauerkraut or tea with raspberry jam or honey or what have you.

On the day the Colonel died I was picking blueberries over on the other side of the hay barn and all at once it felt like a knife'd been pulled out of my cooch, and the awful pain in my crotch, the squeezing feeling in my body that had followed me ever since the first time he ever hit me just flew away.

A GLIMMER OF MORNING creeps between the buildings and onto the garden paths, the roads, the ski trails. A lazy puff of wind swirls over the lake toward the shore carrying bits of dry hay tossed up from a corner of the tar-scented boat dock. The villagers quietly begin to awaken to a new day. Someone steps out onto a porch to look at the thermometer and smells a hint of tar in the air and thinks of the coming spring, when the white drifts will start to melt and little brooks will flow under the crust of snow. The earth will wake into life and begin again to die when the new winter comes.

The Colonel's wife wakes to the smell of wood burned to ash in the stove. She gets up with great difficulty and sits on the edge of her bed. She's bent over with age, as if she had a load of heavy sacks on her back. Her eyes are closed. She hangs her head and gasps for breath. Floats in substanceless darkness.

She sits for a moment, sways, and lies back down again. The fire has gone out, fading into the coals, the warmth fleeing through the cracks in the walls and floor.

This is her fourth life. First was the weekday, Sunday life of her childhood home in a northern town, then the years under the power of the old Colonel, then the shared life with young Tuomas in this house.

Now she's on life's final stretch.

A red trail of blood trickles out of the corner of her mouth onto the reindeer-fur pillow. On the kitchen table are two smoked perch that Tuomas brought her. In the bottom of a basket in the porch pantry there's a lake bream he salted for her. He said he would heat up the big bread oven this week, and broil her some more fish.

Snowflakes drift through the room.

Thanks

Annikki Kariniemi-Willamo-Heikanmaa

and

Anita Seppä, Jonni Aromaa, Jorma Ylävaara, Kirsti Lonka, Mika Kukkonen, Riikka Ala-Harja, Ulla Kautto,

and

Harri Haanpää

ROSA LIKSOM was born in a village of eight houses in Lapland, Finland, where her parents were reindeer breeders and farmers. She spent her youth traveling Europe, living as a squatter and in communes. She won the Finlandia Prize in 2011 for *Compartment No. 6*, which has been translated into thirteen languages. Liksom paints, makes films, and writes in Helsinki.

LOLA ROGERS has translated works by Finland's leading authors of literary and historical fiction, crime fiction, and Finnish Weird. Rogers is an NEA Translation Fellow and a founding member of the Finnish-English Translation Cooperative. She lives in Seattle, Washington.

The text of *The Colonel's Wife* is set in Sabon Next LT Pro.
Book design by Rachel Holscher.
Composition by Bookmobile Design & Digital Publisher Services,
Minneapolis, Minnesota.
Manufactured by Sheridan on acid-free, 30 percent
postconsumer wastepaper.

LIKSOM   1610919
    2019